'The only thi[ng]
contempt.'

Dirk smiled thinly

'That's because you're a conceited oaf. Any good feelings I had about you disappeared long ago.'

'No,' he said thoughtfully. 'I think you enjoyed being hurt. I think you'd prefer it if I took you by force, because then you wouldn't have to admit that you'd lusted after a hated MacAllister. You'd have the sexual pleasure without having to feel guilty about it.'

Dear Reader

As the dark winter nights unfold, what better to turn to than a heart-warming Mills & Boon! As usual, we bring you a selection of books which take you all over the world, with heroines you like and heroes you would love to be with! So take a flight of fancy away from everyday life to the wonderful world of Mills & Boon—you'll be glad you did.

The Editor

Alex Ryder was born and raised in Edinburgh and is married with three sons. She took an interest in writing when, to her utter amazement, she won a national schools competition for a short essay about wild birds. She prefers writing romantic fiction because at heart she's just a big softie. She works now in close collaboration with a scruffy old one-eyed cat who sits on the desk and yawns when she doesn't get it right, but winks when she does.

DARK DECEIVER

BY
ALEX RYDER

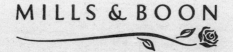

MILLS & BOON LIMITED
ETON HOUSE, 18-24 PARADISE ROAD
RICHMOND, SURREY TW9 1SR

First published in Great Britain 1993
by Mills & Boon Limited

© Alex Ryder 1993

Australian copyright 1993
Philippine copyright 1993
This edition 1993

ISBN 0 263 78303 0

Set in Times Roman 10½ on 12 pt.
01-9312-51177 C

Made and printed in Great Britain

CHAPTER ONE

SHONA stared at the columns of figures in frustration then threw the pen down in disgust. No matter how you looked at it, one thing was nakedly apparent. Another year like the last two and the estate would be bankrupt. Sighing, she went over to the anthracite cooker and poured herself a mug of black coffee.

Her black mood wasn't made any better by the Atlantic gale which was hurling rain at the windows and screaming threats at the solid, granite-built house. The lights in the large, flagstoned kitchen flickered ominously and went out, then, an instant later, the emergency generators in the cellar kicked in and the power came back on. Something else to worry her, she thought. Fuel. When had she last checked the level in the diesel tank? She had no doubt that Morag, her housekeeper, was well stocked with candles and paraffin, but that wasn't the point. It was one thing to be at the mercy of the banks, but to be mocked by the elements at the same time was rubbing salt into the wounds.

Outside it was growing darker, and she glanced at the clock. It was time Lachie was back. Along with his son he'd set off first thing this morning to make sure that the tailrace from Loch Bhuied was clear. With all the rain they'd been having lately there was a danger of the loch overflowing and turning vast acres of valuable grouse moor into useless bog.

Finishing her coffee, she sat down at the polished pine table and went over the accounts once more.

There had to be some way to cut down on expenses, some way to keep things ticking over until this damned recession was over and the rich German and Japanese tourists returned for their packaged hunting, shooting and fishing holidays.

There was one simple solution, of course. It was lying on the table right in front of her—the latest offer from MacAllister's lawyer. Not just an offer, but a clinical assessment of her financial position and future prospects. Just where the hell were they getting their information from? she wondered for the hundredth time. Well, if the offer had come from anyone else she'd have at least thought about it, but she'd cut off her hair and parade naked along Princes Street at one o'clock on a Saturday afternoon before she'd ever let that devil get his hands on her inheritance.

Little good could be said about his ancestors—cattle thieves and cut-throats the lot of them—and Dirk MacAllister, the latest of the line, was just as bad if not worse. He'd never have dared be so presumptuous towards her late father. Rory would have taken that letter and in his own inimitable style have stuffed it down MacAllister's throat.

To be fair, with the amount of money he was offering she could buy herself a luxury service flat in Edinburgh's West End and live a life of indolent pleasure. Then again, he could afford to be generous. Plagues, famines and recessions had never affected the MacAllister clan. They'd always had their fingers in every plum in the orchard.

The hotel and half the houses and shops in Kinvaig belonged to him. So did most of the inshore fishing

fleet in the harbour. There was the Glen Hanish distillery and the fish farm. He even raked in a fortune
from the Government as compensation for not
planting trees in an area deemed to be a place of
'scientific interest'. Only a MacAllister would have
spotted and taken advantage of a piece of stupid
legislation like that.

But the one thing none of the MacAllisters had ever
been able to get their hands on was the Struan property
on their northern border. Centuries ago bloody battles
had been fought over the rights of ownership. Now
the latest of the line was trying to accomplish with an
accountant's pen what his forebears had been unable
to do with musket and claymore.

Anyway, apart from the fact that her father would
leap from his grave in rage if she ever sold out to his
worst enemy, she had a darker, more bitter reason for
hating and despising Dirk MacAllister.

Five long years hadn't wiped away the memory of
the way he'd treated her, nor healed the wound in her
heart. She'd go to her grave cursing the ground he
walked on.

The distant lights of the Land Rover cast a reflection in the window, and she put the accounts away
and called for Morag.

'Lachie will be here in a minute. You can lay the
table now.'

Morag showed her displeasure with a sniff. 'I could
have done it half an hour ago. I don't know why you
can't do your bookkeeping in the library like your
father did instead of getting under my feet all the
time.'

'It's brighter and warmer in here,' she pointed out.
'Anyway, you know as well as I do that Rory would

never have been caught dead in a kitchen. Kitchens are for women.'

'Kitchens are for cooking in. I don't know how often I've told you. In my opinion you're turning out just as stubborn as your father.'

Shona tried to hide her expression of amused exasperation. Only in the Highlands did you find people like Morag, a fiercely independent stock. You might provide them with wages and a roof over their heads, but that never gave you the right to stop them speaking their minds or calling you a fool to your face if they felt like it.

The kitchen door opened, allowing a squall of rain to spatter on the floor, then it slammed shut and Lachie and his teenage son stepped into the light.

The gamekeeper was cradling a fawn in his arms and gently he put it on the floor, where it stood awkwardly on its spindly legs, gazing around curiously at its new surroundings.

She bent down and stroked it gently. 'Poor little thing. Did you get lost, then?' She glanced up at the gamekeeper. 'Where did you find her?'

'Wait till we've eaten, then I'll tell you. It's a long story.' He removed his waxed jacket and battered deerstalker then helped himself to a generous measure of whisky from the bottle in the cupboard. There was a tightly controlled anger on his seamed, weather-beaten face, and she knew better than to press him. She'd find out all in good time.

The rich smell of broth and roast beef filled the kitchen, and as the men ate ravenously she squatted on a cushion on the floor and hand-fed the fawn warm milk from a lemonade bottle fitted with a teat made from a rubber glove.

It was unusual for a fawn to get separated from its mother, but it sometimes happened. The only problem about hand-rearing such a young animal was that they usually became too dependent. They could lose their natural suspicion of humans and when they were eventually sent back to the hills their chances of survival were greatly diminished.

When the meal was finished Lachie got to his feet, retrieved something from his jacket pocket, and laid it on the table.

A cold hand clutched at Shona's heart and the colour drained from her face.

'A crossbow bolt?'

'Aye,' growled Lachie. 'Bloody poachers! That wee beast's mother is dead. I've got her in the back of the Land Rover.'

Cold rage surged through her. This on top of all her other troubles! Closing her eyes and counting to five, she got on top of her emotions and said evenly, 'You'd better tell me what happened.'

'It was young Jamie who spotted them first. We were on our way back from the loch when he saw the red Transit van parked up on the old quarry road. I took a look through the glasses and counted about five of them loading carcasses into the back of the van.'

'They got away with at least three,' said Jamie.

'Aye. Well, we headed up the old road, but they heard us coming. That damn hill's so steep you have to take it in second gear.'

Shona's light blue eyes glittered with the prospect of vengeance. If they'd got away with it this time there was every chance they'd return in a few weeks' time. 'Would you recognise the van again, Lachie?'

'Damn right. Red with a dented back door.' His face darkened. 'Don't worry. I'll be keeping a good look-out for it.'

Neither her gamekeeper nor she worried too much about any of the locals helping themselves to a bit of venison to feed their families when times were bad. It was the organised gangs from down south they detested. These scum were only in it for the money and they often left wounded animals to die in agony.

'I'd better warn MacAllister to be on the look-out for them as well,' Lachie said. He saw her stiffen and he growled, 'There are times when even the worst of enemies have to co-operate for the common good.'

She swallowed her bitterness and shrugged. 'Do what you think is best.'

Lachie told his son to see to the dead beast in the back of the Land Rover, and when the boy had gone he lowered his voice. 'There's something else you should know about MacAllister. I've been meaning to tell you for the last couple of days. I was going to wait till you were in a better mood, but by the looks of things I might be dead of old age by then.'

MacAllister, she thought. If she heard that name one more time she'd scream. She sighed. 'All right. What about him?'

'He's had a surveyor out on Para Mhor. They've been taking measurements.'

At the mention of Para Mhor her heart lurched and the memory of that one insane afternoon rushed like a taunting, gibbering fiend through the secret corridors of her mind. Para Mhor...the howling storm...the fear...then the warmth...the blinding passion and final ecstasy. Then the cold, callous betrayal.

She became aware of Lachie and Morag eyeing her curiously, and she unclenched her fists and forced herself to think calmly over the implications of what she'd just been told.

Para Mhor was an island about half an hour by boat from Kinvaig. A mile long by half a mile wide, it was desolate apart from the ruins of an ancient croft. Too thin-soiled to sustain anything other than whin and machar grass, it was only suitable as pasturage.

The only thing the Struans and MacAllisters had ever agreed about was the futility of fighting over such an unprepossessing piece of real estate. Back in the mists of time they'd reached a tacit agreement that the island would be used as common grazing for sheep during the summer months. After shearing time each clan would transport about fifty of their own sheep by boat and leave them on the island to fend for themselves until late September.

'What would he be needing a surveyor for?' she asked suspiciously.

'Well, it's only a rumour, you understand, but there's talk in Kinvaig of him turning Para Mhor into a holiday resort for the rich tourists. Marina... hotel... chalets.'

Her mouth dropped open in disbelief and she gave an outraged splutter. 'He... he can't do that! Para Mhor isn't his property. It's common grazing. Always has been.'

'Oh, aye? And when was the last time anyone put a sheep on Para Mhor? Not for the last forty years to my knowledge.'

'That isn't the point,' she retorted angrily. 'He should have consulted me first.'

The more she thought about the high-handed action the more furious she became. Lachie was looking at her as if he was sorry he'd ever told her, and he turned to Morag. 'You'd better pour the wee lassie a dram to settle her nerves.'

'I don't need whisky,' she said through clenched teeth. 'I need MacAllister's head on a plate. Who the hell does he think he is? He'd never have dared try a thing like this when my father was alive. I suppose he thinks he can walk all over me.'

'I doubt that,' murmured the gamekeeper. 'When he arrived back in time for old Rory's funeral last year I distinctly remember you threatening to blow his reproductive organs off with a shotgun if he ever set foot on your land again. Not your typical Highland hospitality.'

Morag cackled, 'Aye. And you said it right in front of the Reverend Mr MacLeod. The poor wee man has never been the same since.'

'Rory's funeral would have been an appropriate time for this damned feud to be buried once and for all,' Lachie said drily. 'You're complaining about him not consulting you over Para Mhor. How the devil can he consult you when you won't even answer his phone calls? If you had any sense you'd go and see him right now and find out what he's up to. It would clear the air at least.'

She chewed at her lip and ran her fingers through her short red hair in frustration. Lachie only knew half the story. The hatred she felt for MacAllister wasn't the result of a simple family feud. She'd always taken the old stories her father had told her about the treachery of the MacAllisters with a pinch of salt. She'd been a firm believer in letting bygones be bygones, but that had been before she'd learnt the shattering, sickening truth for herself.

Only she and Dirk MacAllister knew what had happened on that black, infamous day, and he wasn't likely to go broadcasting it to all and sundry.

She'd never really expected him to have the nerve to come back here. After he'd skulked off he'd left his estate in the hands of accountants and an aggressive lout of an estate manager. But on the very day her father had been laid to rest he'd showed up offering sympathy and support.

She'd almost been sick on the spot at his blatant hypocrisy. Was it possible that he'd thought she would have forgotten or forgiven the hurt he'd caused her? No. It was more likely that he imagined she was still the wide-eyed, innocent and foolish little virgin she'd once been. Well, she wasn't foolish any longer. Neither was she a virgin. He'd seen to that.

Morag was placing a blanket by the side of the oven. The fawn would stay indoors for a few days until it had recovered its strength, then it would be allowed out into the walled field at the back.

'Lachie's speaking sense,' she said. 'You don't have to be nice to the man. Just find out what he's up to.'

It dawned on Shona that perhaps she was being too self-centred, allowing her dislike of MacAllister to blind her to the real danger. To tell the truth she didn't give a damn about that desolate island, but if she let him away with this it could be the thin edge of the wedge. Both Lachie and Morag knew that she had her back to the wall already, and they were bound to be wondering what would happen to them if she was forced to relinquish control. Neither of them was getting any younger. Their long service and loyalty demanded that she do something to stop the rot.

'Do you really think that he can get away with building on Para Mhor?' she asked her gamekeeper.

He shrugged. 'I wouldn't know. That's a matter that you'd better take up with your lawyer in Edinburgh. Common grazing rights is a pretty well established custom in the Western Highlands, but I dare say a clever man could find some way round them.'

Making up her mind, she said, 'Right! I'll see him tomorrow and demand that...' No! If she waited until tomorrow she'd just lie in her bed simmering away angrily all night. Rory wouldn't have put it off for one second. 'No, dammit! I'll go right now.'

'Looking like that?' sniffed Morag.

'Looking like what?' she demanded. She looked down at herself, at the baggy, washed-out Aran sweater and jeans tucked into scuffed leather boots. 'I suppose I should wear my cashmere suit, patent court shoes, pearls and matching accessories?'

'There's no call for sarcasm,' Morag said huffily. 'What I mean is that if you're going to that big house you never know who you'll meet. I hear the place is always full of his society friends from down south. You don't want them thinking the Struans is nothing more than a bunch of scruffy tinkers, do you?'

Morag's sudden outburst of uncharacteristic snobbery riled her and she snapped, 'They can think what they damn well like. I'm not interested in the opinions of his aristocratic cronies.'

'Aye...' muttered Morag. 'Just as stubborn as your father. I might have known better.'

Lachie reached for her coat. 'I'll run you there in the Land Rover.'

'Never mind. You've been out since early morning. You've had a hard enough day as it is. I'll take the jeep. It's easier for me to handle.'

He looked relieved, whether at not having to drive another five miles through the storm or not having to witness the confrontation between her and MacAllister she wasn't quite sure. In any case, it didn't matter. She wanted to be on her own when she met MacAllister. Things might be said between them that she wanted no one else to hear.

The rain drummed on the canvas top of the jeep and the headlights lanced through the gloom as she set off on the treacherous road around the bay. On her right the sea hurled itself across the rocky foreshore, sending torrents of sea-spray across her windscreen.

When she passed through the fishing village of Kinvaig it was closed and shuttered against the wind and rain, its one main street deserted. A handful of fishing-boats—sixty-foot Seine netters—bobbed in the harbour. On a night like this the whole West Coast fishing fleet would be finding sanctuary in every port from Scourie to the Clyde, and if the storm lasted a few more days the housewives in Glasgow and Edinburgh would be complaining because the price of white fish had gone up a few pence.

She dropped a gear as the jeep began to climb up to the high moor on the southern side of the bay. Now the road was straighter but the wind was even fiercer.

Grimly she stared through the windscreen, her eyes smouldering as she remembered the last time she'd come along this road. The sun had been shining that day, and life had seemed so wonderful...

She'd stepped out of the village store, unheedingly flicking through the pages of her magazine, and it was only by sheer luck and the driver's reflexes that the car had managed to stop in time. There'd been a screech of brakes and a smell of burning rubber and her heart had leapt to her mouth.

He'd got out of the car, his features dark with anger, and grabbed her roughly by the shoulder. 'What the hell do you think you're playing at? Has no one ever told you to...?' His voice trailed off and he frowned at her. 'Shona? Shona Struan? Is it really you?'

She got her breath back. 'I...I'm sorry, Mr MacAllister. It was a stupid thing to do.'

The anger had gone from his lean, finely chiselled features, and his light grey eyes were wide and quizzical, as if they could hardly believe what they were seeing.

She was acutely conscious of the way the breeze was moulding her light cotton dress to the contours of her body, and she felt a little apprehensive as he looked her over with obvious appreciation.

He grinned, showing white, even teeth. 'The last time I saw you you were all elbows and knees and sucking a lollipop.'

She felt herself colouring. 'Hardly. I was eighteen when I left here to go to university. You were probably too busy to notice. I seem to recall that you were engaged to be married at the time. Some society butterfly from Edinburgh, wasn't it?' Almost immediately she wondered why she'd said that. After all, it hadn't been any of her business.

His grey eyes widened a fraction, then he smiled affably. 'You're quite right. A scatter-brain. She eventually decided that life here was too laid-back for her sophisticated tastes. Missed the theatres and restaurants and discos. I sincerely hope that your sojourn in the bright lights hasn't soured your love of the simple life.'

'I was too busy studying to have time for theatres and restaurants,' she said coolly. 'Besides, I was born and bred here.'

He grinned in approval. 'Just as I was. Which just goes to prove that we natives should stick together.'

She wondered vaguely what he meant by that remark. If she didn't know any better she'd have sworn that he was making a pass at her. She was well aware of her own attractions. If you liked red hair, that was. She was reasonably nice-looking and she'd never been ashamed of her figure. Plenty of men at university, including a few of the lecturers and one particularly randy old professor, had indicated a desire to get to know her better, and not just on an intellectual level. But Dirk MacAllister? That would have been a real surprise.

She well remembered having a teenage crush on him when she was fifteen. All very secret and embarrassing, of course, and something only to be fantasised about on warm, restless nights. She'd thought him terribly handsome and sophisticated, and she'd been a little in awe of the respect he seemed to command in the village. But he'd been an old man! Twenty-five at least! And he'd always seemed to have some beautiful creature straight from the pages of a fashion magazine hanging on to his arm. It was hardly surprising that he'd paid her not the slightest bit of attention.

But now she was twenty and he'd be only thirty and her own blossomed maturity had ironed out the age difference.

Looking at him now, she could see that there was more to him than classic good looks. There was something about him that made an impact on a more subliminal level. Body language, perhaps. Or the deep, masculine resonance of his voice. A hundred generations of Celtic breeding had given him all the command and self-assurance of a man born to power and wealth. It took little imagination to picture him as some young warrior erect on a wild stallion, sword in hand and eyes blazing defiance at anyone who dared challenge his birthright.

What it all added up to was some inexplicable yet potent sexual attraction that was almost frightening in its intensity. Love him or hate him, no woman on earth could possibly have ignored him, and she had certainly never met a man who made her intrigued and frightened at the same time. She tore her gaze away quickly and said shakily, 'I...I'd better go now.'

His hand reached out, touching the bare flesh of her upper arm, and the gentle contact sent tiny impulses racing through her nervous system. 'What's your hurry, Shona?' His grey eyes almost but didn't quite taunt her. 'Afraid your father will find out you've been consorting with the enemy?'

The idea had never entered her head, but now that he'd mentioned it she became aware of a conflict between loyalty to her father and the need to demonstrate her independence of thought and freedom of action.

'I decide who my enemies are, Mr MacAllister. Not my father,' she informed him calmly.

The breeze, which was still turning her dress into a piece of opaque cling film, ruffled his dark hair, and once again his eyes registered approval. 'In that case you may call me Dirk. I'm tired of people calling me MacAllister all the time. It makes me sound very unapproachable. Contrary to what you may have heard, I don't eat babies or throw old widows out into the snow.' He paused then removed his hand from her arm and nodded in the direction of the hotel. 'I'd like to buy you lunch, if I may. As long as you aren't afraid of causing a lot of gossip, which no doubt there will be.'

He was at it again, she thought, the challenge lightly cloaked in an innocent-sounding invitation. Or was it just her imagination that was making her suspicious, years of brainwashing and listening to old tales?

'Thanks. I would, but I'm not particularly hungry at the moment.' It was a feeble prevarication and she felt annoyed at herself for opting for the easy way out.

'I'm sure you can manage a bite at least,' he cajoled softly. 'Besides, I hate eating alone and I'd like to hear how you got on at university.'

The rejection of such a polite invitation could be viewed at best as bad manners and in such a closed society as this might even be regarded as downright hostility. If she was really serious about having nothing to do with this centuries-old feud the sooner she nailed her colours to the mast the better. Let the locals gossip. Why should she care? It was a free country and she'd damn well be sociable to anyone she wanted. Deep down she hoped she'd find the nerve some day to tell that to her father.

Ten minutes later, as they sat in the deserted dining-room, he eyed her with amusement as she helped herself to another plateful of cold cuts. 'I thought you weren't hungry? At least I'm glad to see you aren't one of the brown rice and spinach brigade. I like a woman with a healthy appetite.'

She wasn't quite sure how to take that. Was it a compliment or a sarcastic comment on the amount of food on the plate? She sliced delicately at a piece of chicken breast and decided to give him the benefit of the doubt.

'So what were you studying at university?' he asked with unfeigned interest.

'Estate management and accounting.'

He nodded and looked at her thoughtfully. 'Then you intend staying here to help your father run the estate?'

The question took her by surprise. 'Of course. It'll be mine one day. I wouldn't dream of leaving here. It's my home.'

His face took on a smile of genuine pleasure. 'I'm glad about that. And I admire your commitment to family duty. But I'd better warn you that it's no bed of roses you're going into. I should know. Things are bad at the moment and they're going to get worse.'

She dismissed his warning airily. 'I'm not afraid of hard work.'

'The Struans never were. But sometimes hard work isn't enough.'

Trying not to appear smug, she told him, 'I'm aware of that. But I have plans.'

His mouth quirked—a little too patronisingly, she thought. 'Good for you. Have you discussed these plans with your father?'

'Not yet,' she admitted cautiously. 'I'm waiting for the right moment.'

His eyebrows rose and his voice became dry. 'Then you may still be waiting ten years from now. Your father isn't the kind of man who's receptive to any kind of innovation. He's still trying to come to terms with the internal combustion engine.'

Tightening her lips, she got to her feet and said coldly, 'Thanks for the meal, Mr MacAllister. I really must be going now.'

He remained seated, his grey eyes reflecting the disappointment in his voice. 'That's a great pity, Shona. I've no wish to quarrel with you. This foolish business between our families has gone on long enough. I'd really hoped that——'

'I know it's gone on long enough,' she broke in stiffly. 'But I won't stay here and listen to you insult my father.'

'I'm not insulting him,' he said calmly. 'I'm simply stating a fact, and you know it. But if you won't face up to reality, then this undeclared war will go on forever. You really don't want that, do you?'

'No. But——'

'Never mind the buts. Sit down, and we'll discuss this like two civilised people. If it makes you feel any better, my father is just the same as yours. Next year he's retiring and I'll be in charge, and I intend making a few changes around here.'

Grudgingly she regained her seat. He could have a point. It was only family loyalty that had made her

leap to the defence of her father, not any great admiration for the way he ran the estate.

'That's better.' He grinned. 'I've a feeling that you
and I are going to become the best of friends, Shona.'

She looked back at him impassively, although her
mind was pondering over his statement. What exactly
did he mean by 'best of friends'? The way he'd looked
her over when they'd first met showed that he had
something more basic in mind. She was no fool.
Neither was she cold-blooded, and she'd be lying to
herself if she didn't admit that she was flattered.

'There's no reason why you and I can't work
together,' he went on persuasively. 'We'd be stupid to
perpetuate the mistakes of our ancestors. Don't you
agree?'

'I can hardly disagree if you put it like that,' she
murmured. 'I'm all for peace and harmony. It's not
me you have to convince. It's Rory.'

'Rory will have to loosen his grip on the reins sooner
or later,' he pointed out quietly. 'But even before then
he'll come to rely on your advice more and more. I
know that may sound a bit callous and even dis-
respectful, but that doesn't alter the facts.' He
shrugged. 'Who knows? Perhaps you might be able
to persuade him that instead of our families squab-
bling all the time we should be uniting to fight the
common enemy.'

She frowned. 'At the risk of appearing stupid, could
you enlighten me as to who our common enemy is?
Don't tell me we're going to form an alliance to fight
the Argyle Campbells.'

He gave a deep chuckle. 'Hardly. The Campbells
are nothing compared to the financial institutions and
foreign syndicates who are raping the Highlands right

now and seem intent on turning the whole damned place into a gigantic theme park complete with bingo and candy-floss stalls.'

She smiled in spite of herself. 'You sound just like Rory. I've heard him say the same thing himself.'

'Of course you have. You're father isn't a fool. But he thinks he can do it on his own. Or he'd like to think he could, because it's inconceivable to him to ever dream of joining forces with a hated MacAllister.'

There was nothing he'd said so far that she could find fault with. He'd been polite and honest about his intentions and hadn't been too heavy with the condescension bit, so when he offered his hand over the table to seal their understanding she didn't hesitate.

His grip was warm and she could almost feel his strength passing through her arm as he looked deeply into her eyes. 'Are we friends?'

Her chest felt just a little tight as she murmured, 'Friends.'

He gave her hand a final, gentle squeeze then chuckled. 'This must be some sort of record. I wonder if we're the first of our families ever to shake hands over anything.'

Outside the hotel he surveyed the quiet road. 'Where's your transport?'

The sun was warm on her back and over the harbour the gulls were wheeling in lazy circles. 'I walked,' she told him. 'It's such a nice day.'

'Well, I'd better drive you home. I'd like a word with Rory, anyway. That's if he'll take the time to see me.'

'You're out of luck,' she told him. 'He's gone to the cattle auction in Inverness. He usually gets back about midnight.' She smiled brightly. 'Anyway, I don't want to go back yet. Morag is busy with the spring-cleaning. She almost chased me out of the house this morning to stop me getting in her way. I'm just going to sit on the pier, breathing in this wonderful air and getting used to the place again after the rush and noise of Glasgow.'

His grey eyes studied her thoughtfully. 'I'm going out to Para Mhor. You can come along if you like.'

The thought of a boat trip appealed to her, but she didn't want to appear too eager in case he got the wrong idea. 'Oh, I don't know. There's nothing much to see on Para Mhor, is there?'

'One of our boats was driven ashore by a gale last week. I'm going out to see if it's worth salvaging. It should be more interesting than sitting on the pier watching gulls.'

She smiled hesitantly. 'All right. You've talked me into it.'

'Good.' He took her firmly by the arm and led her to his car. 'First I have to go home and change. While I'm at it, we'll see if we can find you an oilskin jacket.'

His car was too powerful for the roads up here. A younger man would have taken the opportunity to impress her by pushing the needle up to seventy, but he kept to a safe and comfortable forty. A man like him didn't have to prove anything. He let his personality and charm do all the work.

Considering everything, she wasn't surprised that she was beginning to like this man who was supposed to be her mortal enemy.

His father was an unknown quantity, however, and she voiced her misgivings about the reception she might receive as they neared the house.

'You don't have to worry about him,' Dirk assured her with a touch of bitterness. 'He's having another drying-out session at a private clinic in Edinburgh. At least the distillery has started making a profit again.'

They pulled up in the front drive and as he came round to open her door she shook her head. 'I'd rather stay here, if you don't mind.'

He took one look at the adamant set to her mouth then he shrugged. 'OK. I'll be as quick as I can.'

She knew she was being irrational, but there was something about the house that intimidated her. There was a brooding, threatening aspect to the dark, ivy-covered walls and the crenellated roof. It reminded her of some grim fortress rather than a place to live. It was a relic of a bygone age. She was glad when Dirk emerged about five minutes later and restarted the car.

It was windier once they'd left the shelter of the harbour, and she was glad of the oilskin jacket to protect her from the spray as the powerful boat headed towards the island.

There was too much noise from the outboard engine to carry on a conversation and she contented herself by watching the competent way Dirk handled the craft. Beneath his oilskin he was now wearing an open-necked checked shirt and canvas jeans. Hatless, his dark hair streamed in the wind, and his eyes were narrowed in the reflected glare from the sea. His distant ancestors must have looked much the same as they fought the Viking long-ships, she thought.

As they approached the island he pointed and she saw the grounded fishing boat lying precariously on the rocks.

After tying up at the dilapidated jetty they removed their jackets, then Dirk helped her out of the boat. Together they walked along the shoreline until they came to the wreck, and Dirk got down on his haunches to examine the keel.

Finally he shook his head. 'The timbers are too far gone. The next storm will probably drag her off the rocks and finish her.' He stood up regretfully. 'The crew managed to save most of the gear as they were being rescued, but I'd better go aboard and make sure.' He paused and looked at her doubtfully. 'It may be a bit dangerous...'

She could take a hint and she said, 'Don't worry. I won't get in your way. I think I'll go exploring. See you later.'

Climbing up the steep incline, she stood for a moment surveying the flat landscape. About three quarters of a mile to the north she could see the ruined croft, the only sign that the island had ever been inhabited. Deciding to go and investigate, she began walking towards it, quite unaware that one of the worst storms in living memory was about to strike.

CHAPTER TWO

THE MacAllister house was just as she remembered it. In the headlights of the jeep it seemed to draw itself erect like some mythological creature of stone, daring her to come any closer.

She switched off the engine, doused the lights, then forced the jeep door open against the driving wind and rain. Refusing to cower before the imagined wrath of the house and the very real wrath of the storm, she marched the few yards to the front door and heaved on the old-fashioned bell-pull.

An overhead light was switched on and a moment later the door was cautiously opened by a stout, matronly woman wearing a dark housecoat and a suspicious expression. Obviously this wasn't a night for social visits. She peered through the rain for a moment then raised her hands. 'Shona! Shona Struan! It is you, isn't it?'

'Aye. It's me, Mrs Ross,' she said grimly. 'Is Dirk at home?'

For a moment the housekeeper looked nonplussed, then she stammered, 'You ... you'd better come in. You're getting soaked.'

Shona stepped into the hallway and the housekeeper continued to stare at her. A Struan calling at this house? It had never happened before. At last she got her wits together and said, 'He's in the library. I'll tell him you're here.'

The water was already pooling on the parquet flooring at Shona's feet. She removed her coat, hung it on the hallstand, then caught sight of her reflection in the mirror. Dammit! She should have worn a hat. Her hair was plastered to her forehead and her nose was red and shiny. But her anger hadn't been dampened. If anything the fires had been stoked even further.

The vast hallway with its dark panelling seemed cold and gloomy. On her left a wide staircase led to the upper floors, which were in darkness. From here the house didn't look any friendlier than it had from the outside.

Her patience was wearing thin by the time the housekeeper returned, and she looked at her in irritation. 'Well?'

'He's busy at the moment. He wonders if you wouldn't mind waiting.' Mrs Ross was apologetic.

Shona drew in her breath as a cold lump of anger rose within her and she resisted the impulse to barge past the housekeeper and find MacAllister for herself. Forcing her to cool her heels was the kind of calculated insult she should have expected from the likes of him. It was his childish way of telling her that there was nothing she had to say that could possibly be of any interest to him. Well, they'd see about that!

'Come through to the kitchen,' said Mrs Ross. 'It's nice and warm and I've just made a big pot of tea.'

She eyed the housekeeper belligerently, then sighed. It wasn't Mrs Ross's fault and it would be unfair to vent her anger on her. She must have had a bad enough time as it was having to work for that cretin of a man. She managed a smile. 'Thanks, Mrs Ross. That's very kind of you.'

'Aye... Well, I'm sure he won't keep you waiting long. Meanwhile you can dry yourself off.'

Reluctantly she let herself be led through the hall towards the rear of the house. Expecting to be confronted with a dreary, Victorian relic of a scullery, she was surprised to find herself in a brightly lit, modern kitchen that wouldn't have disgraced a five-star hotel. It had colourful ceramic-tiled walls and worktops of gleaming stainless steel. No ancient Aga here, but a huge electric cooking range and a food preparation area equipped with every gadget known to modern technology. She thought of her own kitchen back home and winced. Poor old Morag would have been struck dumb at the sight of this place. Still... Perhaps when things picked up and she could afford it...

Mrs Ross switched on an electric heater then handed her a towel. 'Dry your hair and I'll pour some tea.'

A few minutes later the chill began to leave her bones as she sat by the heater, a mug of hot, sweet tea laced with whisky clasped in her hands. As if sensing that she was in no mood for idle gossip, Mrs Ross left her alone and busied herself at the far end of the kitchen.

Shona sipped at the tea and her blue eyes reflected her bitterness as her thoughts returned once more to that fateful day so long ago on Para Mhor.

The storm hit suddenly and took her completely unprepared. One moment the sky above was a brilliant blue, then a chill wind cut through her cotton dress. The sky darkened and she looked up to see the thick curtain of rain-swollen clouds obliterate the sun. As the first drops of rain fell she stood for a moment in indecision. Should she carry on or go back and shelter in the fishing-boat? The croft looked nearer, so she made up her mind and began to run over the now slippery grass. It was too late now to regret not bringing the oilskin jacket, and if she got soaked it would be her own fault.

She'd covered about fifty yards when there was a blinding flash followed almost immediately by a horrendous clap of thunder. The wind was gathering strength, hurling the rain to sting her body painfully through her thin dress. Gasping, she continued to stumble forward, her head bent towards the ground. When next she looked up, the croft was no longer visible through the sheets of water that blurred her vision and ran in rivulets down the back of her neck.

There was another terrifying flash and explosion and she saw a whin bush about fifty yards away disappear in a huge ball of orange fire. Panic-stricken, she still had enough sense to throw herself flat on the ground, where she wouldn't present such a tempting target to the lightning. Her skin prickled with fear and her heart fluttered like a frightened bird. She'd seen freak storms before, but nothing as vicious as this. You could expect them during a hot, prolonged summer, but never at this time of the year.

The seconds ticked by and she moved her lips in silent prayer while the gale screeched mockingly in her ear, then there was one silent, blinding flash of light and she lost consciousness.

It returned slowly. Someone was shaking her and rubbing her hands and she heard the strangely muffled voice telling her to wake up. She didn't want to wake up. She just wanted to sleep. 'Go 'way,' she mumbled.

'Come on, Shona. Waken up.'

He was shaking her violently now and she opened her eyes. She was in the croft, sitting on the floor with her back against the wall, and Dirk was on his knees beside her. She swallowed two or three times and the buzzing noise in her ears stopped, but she could still hear the sound of the raging storm outside. 'Wh . . . what happened?'

'I found you lying on the ground. Are you all right?'

'You're all wet,' she mumbled.

'Never mind me. Do you realise that you were almost killed?'

It came back to her now and her eyes opened wide. 'The lightning!'

'It missed you by a couple of yards. There's a huge circle of burnt grass. God! When I saw you lying there . . .'

She shivered. Outside, the lightning was still flickering and discharging bolts of destructive energy at the island. She tried to struggle to her feet, but he restrained her. 'Stay there. I'm going to light a fire before you catch pneumonia.'

It was good advice, because she still felt dizzy. She gazed around her. The roof was leaking in one or two places, but it was dry at this end of the room.

Dirk had started ripping up the floorboards and smashing them into kindling. Over his shoulder he explained to her, 'When the storm started I realised that you didn't have your oilskin jacket so I came after you. It's by your side there. As soon as I get this fire going I want you out of those wet clothes.'

She turned that prospect over in her mind and was about to voice a feeble protest when another, even more uncomfortable thought occurred to her. With a wind like this the sea would be far too rough to make the crossing back to the mainland. Supposing they were stranded here for the night? She could imagine what her father would have to say about that!

'I don't think this weather will last long,' he said when she put the point to him. 'There was nothing about it on the shipping forecast this morning. God knows where it came from—a hole in the ozone layer for all I know. It's just a localised freak. With any luck it'll all be over in two or three hours.'

He finally got a good blaze going in the fireplace and he helped her to her feet.

'Thanks,' she murmured. Her soaked dress was clinging to her skin, leaving nothing to anyone's imagination, and she became all too aware of the look of hungry speculation in his eyes.

'Thanks?' he repeated softly. 'Is that all I get?' His hand went around her waist, drawing her closer. 'Especially when you have so much to offer.'

She was suddenly caught in a slow-moving vortex of muddled sensations, mostly a mixture of excitement and mouth-drying fear. In spite of her attempt to sound casual her voice had a betraying tremble. 'What did you have in mind?'

His mouth was now dangerously close to hers. 'A kiss to begin with, Shona. You can surely spare that.'

She tried a light-hearted smile. Perhaps if she made a joke out of it and kept the mood light and bantering it wouldn't go any further. 'Well . . . if it'll make you feel any better.'

'It will,' he assured her with an anticipatory grin. 'Ever since I've seen how grown-up and bewitching you've become I've been wanting to taste that delicious mouth of yours.'

His arm flexed, pulling her soft, yielding body against his own, and his lips fastened themselves firmly over hers.

At that first warm, moist contact every instinct warned her to remain passive and unresponsive, but the slow, sensual movement of his mouth gliding over hers undermined her resolve. Oh, God! It was such a wonderful sensation. Never had a kiss been so tantalising, so sweetly and passionately arousing. Unheeding of the consequences, her hands reached up and entwined themselves around his neck, and as she stood on tiptoe her body arced itself even harder against his.

She could feel the steady thud of his pounding heart in her own breast, and his lips left hers to brush lightly over her closed eyelids.

'God, Shona! You're so beautiful,' he whispered. 'It's unbelievable. How did I never notice it before you left? Was I blind?'

His left hand came up to caress the nape of her neck and his lips nuzzled at the smooth, sensitive skin below her ear.

Cold reason told her to push him away, because she knew the inevitable end if she didn't put a stop to this now, but as his right hand cupped her breast reason drowned in a sea of sensual gratification. Her nipples had ripened in expectation and she had that weak, liquid feeling in her loins. Other men had taken her in their arms, but their clumsy efforts to arouse her had disgusted her and put her off. But Dirk was different. He was a master musician who knew the right notes and the chords to play. His voice wasn't harsh with selfish desire but soft and darkly shaded with the promise of shared fulfilment.

Gently he unbuttoned the top of her dress then released her breasts from the confines of her bra.
Bending down, he took a nipple gently between his
lips, inflaming her senses and sending tremors of delight the length of her body.

Straightening up, he kissed her on the mouth again
then looked directly into her blue eyes and announced, 'I want you, Shona. I'm going to make love
to you. Here. Now.'

The calm, straightforward declaration of his intentions neither offended her nor took her by surprise.
It was the natural culmination of all that had happened since she'd agreed to have lunch with him barely
two hours ago. Whether she should have tried to
prevent it going this far was neither here nor there.
She was powerless, because her need was suddenly as
fierce and demanding as his own, a need that she'd
suppressed for too long. Suppressed until . . . until he
had been ready to take her? It was a curious thought,
yet why had she rejected all other would-be lovers?
Had he been in her subconscious all these years,
awaiting this moment in time?

He'd been watching the play of emotions on her
face and now he raised a slightly mocking brow.
'Perhaps you object? After all, I am one of the hated
MacAllisters.'

The accusation horrified her and she hastened to
assure him, 'How can you say that, Dirk? I've nothing
against you because of your name. I thought you believed that.'

He considered her answer and its implication, then
smiled in satisfaction. Cupping her cheeks in the palms
of his hands, he said softly, 'We're fitting partners,
Shona, the end-product of two proud and historic

blood lines. I've a feeling it was all leading up to this moment.'

His fingers slowly began undoing the rest of her buttons and she stood silent and immobile, doing nothing to hinder him. Finally he slid the dress gently over her shoulders and it flopped damply to the ground.

Her bra was next to go. In the light of the fire her skin glowed soft and golden and she felt no shame as his eyes devoured her in reverential silence. Slowly he reached out to cup a breast in each hand, then with a reckless hunger his mouth once more sought the ripeness of her lips.

Sated at last with the sweetness of her mouth, he stepped back and removed his shirt. With his eyes locked on hers he completed his undressing then gave a harsh command. 'Look at me, Shona. There'll be no shame or mock-modesty between us. We should savour the sight of each other as well as the touch.'

Obedient to his command, she allowed her gaze to travel downwards, past the broad shoulders, deep chest and hard-ridged muscles of his stomach. Then lower until at last her voice escaped in a trembling sigh of wonder.

'Well?' he teased softly. 'Does it please you to see the effect you have on me?'

Without waiting for an answer, he dropped to his knees before her and slowly eased her nylon briefs down past her hips and the silky-smooth length of her legs, then, reaching up to her waist, he pulled her down beside him. Arranging the cast-off clothes as a makeshift bed, he eased her sideways until they were lying together.

Once again his hands began an unbearable orchestration of sensual pleasure over the dips and contours of her body. With her breath rasping in her throat and her heart now hammering dementedly in her ears, she squirmed and arced her body closer to his. The taste and smell of him filled her senses and stoked the fire of her passion.

He rolled her on to her back then eased himself on top of her, then with one hand at the base of her spine he moulded her towards him until their bodies became one.

Suddenly he paused, a look of surprise and wonder on his face, then, driven by a force he could no longer control, he gave one hard thrust. The brief moment of sharp pain was forgotten, and tiny moans and sighs escaped her throat as her body responded to the slow, rhythmic motion. She squeezed her eyes shut at the feeling of unbearable pleasure, and as the music of their lovemaking became faster and reached the final, shattering crescendo she shuddered and bit sweetly into his shoulder.

Inevitably the force of her passion dissolved to leave a feeling of sweet, warm exhaustion, and for a while they lay still and contented in each other's arms. His fingers ran gently through her hair and his lips pressed themselves against her closed eyes.

Finally he eased his crushing weight off her prostrate form, then got to his knees and stared down at her. Her smile of contented satiety was replaced by a worried frown as she saw the lines of anger etched on the bleak angles of his face. The thought that somehow she'd not come up to his expectations was galling to her pride, and her voice trembled.

'Wh...what's wrong, Dirk? Why are you looking like that?'

'For God's sake, Shona! Why didn't you tell me?'

His voice was a harsh accusation, and it took a moment for the cause of his anger to become all too apparent. She turned her head away in shame and bit her lip. The feeling of guilt didn't last. After all, it was nothing to be ashamed of.

'I thought you knew,' she said, her eyes and voice suddenly defiant. 'I suppose you're one of those people who automatically equate student life with promiscuity. Well, I'm sorry if it's upset you, but I'd have thought it would give you cause for self-congratulation. Isn't it every man's ambition to take a girl's virginity?' She paused, then challenged him with a mocking smile. 'When you did find out it didn't stop you going ahead, did it?'

His eyes widened in surprise at her outburst, then he laughed. 'By God, Shona! You're right. I'm an evil-minded chauvinist pig and I don't deserve someone like you.'

She relaxed again. Stretching her arms upwards, she forgave him with a smile and murmured, 'Then come and lie beside me, you big pig, and keep me warm.'

Outside the storm still raged, but, safe and contented in his arms, she closed her eyes drowsily.

It was some time later when she awoke. He was busy putting more wood on the fire and she watched lazily through half-closed eyes at the way his muscles and sinews rippled beneath the satin-smooth skin of his back and legs. He was like some lithe, predatory lord of the jungle, she thought.

He turned, saw that she was awake, and grinned. She raised herself on one elbow then suppressed a giggle. 'Look at the state you're in. Are you still not satisfied?'

He glanced down at himself then shrugged. 'Don't blame me. It has a mind of its own.'

The blood began to heat up in her veins again and she tossed her head. 'Then you'd better lie down again and we'll see what we can do about it.'

By six that evening the storm had blown itself out and the sea was once more calm enough to make the crossing.

Her hair was a mess and her dress, although dry, was creased and showing signs of hard wear. That alone was enough to draw more than a few speculative glances when they stepped on to the pier at Kinvaig, but she ignored them.

Dirk ran her home in his car, but at her insistence he parked out of sight of the house. Sooner or later Morag would hear through the local grape-vine that she'd spent the day with Dirk, but for the moment she didn't feel like answering too many awkward questions.

Dirk switched off the engine, then sat drumming his fingers thoughtfully on the steering-wheel. He hadn't spoken much at all since they'd left Para Mhor, and she wondered what he was thinking about.

A diplomatic way of saying, Wham, bam, thank you, ma'am, perhaps?

This afternoon had been more than just a wildly abandoned display of passion. It had been a lesson to her in more ways than one. Dirk and she were both savage Highlanders at heart, it seemed. The genes of their pagan Celtic ancestors still swam in their blood and sexual attraction for each other had surged through the Calvinistic crust of civilised behaviour.

But she had neither regrets nor feelings of shame. There were times when she was short-tempered or stupid or impetuous, but no one was going to accuse her of hypocrisy. That was the greatest sin of all.

Dirk had used her and she had used him, both for their own gratification, so she could claim no moral hold over him. Nevertheless she wished he just wouldn't sit there without talking.

Finally the silence became embarrassing and she undid her seatbelt and said lightly, 'Well, I suppose you want to get home now and carve another notch on your belt.'

Her remark at least provoked him into an instant response, and he looked at her sharply. 'Is that all you think of me?'

'What am I supposed to think?' she challenged. 'I recognise that "party's over" look when I see it. But you might at least say goodbye. After all, you are supposed to be a gentleman.'

'You're going to break a leg one day if you don't stop jumping to conclusions,' he growled. 'And any more talk about notches on belts and I might just take one to your backside.'

She reached for the door-handle. 'In that case I'd better go now. I'm not into that kind of stuff.'

He grinned and caught her arm, restraining her. 'Stay where you are. We've got to decide what to do.'

She frowned. 'Do about what?'

'About you, for God's sake! Has it occurred to you that you might be pregnant?'

'Of course it's occurred to me,' she answered a little drily. 'I'm a country girl, remember? I knew the facts of life when I was five years old.'

'And it doesn't worry you?' he asked, apparently intrigued by her calm acceptance.

She shrugged. 'There's time enough to start worrying when I know for certain.' That was a lie. She was worried stiff right now, but she had too much pride to let him see it.

Her father was going to be the big problem. If it turned out that she was pregnant he would be disappointed in her for being so foolish as to let it happen, but he'd accept the situation. Highlanders like him had always had an earthy tolerance and understanding about passion and the temptations of the flesh. But if he discovered that it was a MacAllister child she was carrying...! That was something she didn't want to think about right now.

With what sounded like a remarkable lack of enthusiasm he drawled, 'I suppose it would be a waste of time asking you to marry me.'

'Yes. It probably would,' she retorted, stung by his tone. 'If I thought you were really serious I might give it some consideration. But if it's just your idea of "doing the decent thing by me" you can forget it. I wouldn't take any man on those terms.'

'So you admit that a MacAllister is capable of being "decent"?'

Her voice came out a lot sharper than she'd intended. 'I never thought otherwise. If I had I'd never even have agreed to have lunch with you.' Her feeling of well-being and warmth was being blown away in the icy wind of cold reality. It looked as if the party really was over. Well, she really had nothing to complain about. When she'd gone into Kinvaig that morning it hadn't been with the intention of shopping for a husband.

Her mood of dejection wasn't improved by the blatant cynicism of his next question. 'Then I can be sure that your father isn't going to come looking for me with a marriage licence in one hand and a shotgun in the other?'

She threw him a look of contempt. 'Don't worry. If I do have anything to tell him I'll keep your name well out of it.'

'Hmm . . .' he said thoughtfully. 'Then I'll just have to tell him myself.'

Her eyes widened in confusion over his complete turn around. 'What did you say?'

'I said that I'd have to tell him myself. Someone has to.' He regarded the look of amazement on her face with amusement. 'Once that's out of the way we can start making arrangements for the wedding.'

'W . . . wedding?' Was he trying to make a fool of her? she wondered.

'Aye,' he said drily. 'Church bells . . . guests . . . honeymoon. They're quite common. People get married all the time.'

Ignoring the mild sarcasm, she swallowed. 'W . . . what makes you think I want to marry you?'

'Because you said that you'd consider it if you were sure that I was being serious. Well, I am serious and I don't give a damn whether you're pregnant or not this time. I happen to be in love with you, so you'd better start considering.'

She managed to unstick her tongue from the roof of her mouth. 'This . . . this is a bit sudden, Dirk.' As soon as she'd said it she felt like groaning. Imagine coming out with an old cliché like that! Then in her confusion she came out with another. 'You . . . you hardly know me.' God! This was ridiculous. Why couldn't she think of something original to say?

He lifted her hand to his mouth and gently bit the fleshy mound at the base of her thumb. 'I've just found out all I need to know, Shona. You've got self-respect and courage.' He grinned then added wickedly, 'And enough sex appeal to drive a man insane.'

She gulped, wondering what to say next. He was waiting for an answer, but his very nearness was denying her the ability of rational thought. That blazing, charismatic power was already working its insidious magic on her hormones. No one had ever been able to make her feel so pulsatingly alive and aware of her own body, and no one else was ever likely to. The decision was almost out of her hands.

'All right, Dirk,' she whispered. 'I'll be your wife.'

He leaned closer and pressed his mouth on hers in a lingering, warm and delicious kiss until she pushed him away and struggled for breath.

Staring unseeingly through the windscreen she murmured, 'I don't know what my father will say about this. His only daughter marrying a MacAllister! He'll have a fit.'

Dirk nodded grimly. 'That's only to be expected. My own father won't be celebrating at the prospect either. But I can handle him. Anyway, there's nothing either of them can do about it. The age of the dinosaurs is over.'

'You don't know Rory as well as I do,' she said bleakly.

'No. But he isn't a fool. Once he realises how we feel about each other he might decide to bury the hatchet for good. He might have mellowed with age.'

She shook her head. 'Oak trees don't mellow with age. They just get harder to cut down. I'd better talk to him first, prepare the ground for you.'

He didn't answer, but the more she thought about it the better the idea seemed. Rory would rant and rave and stamp his great feet and rattle the china with his thumping, but he'd eventually calm down. Then he'd sulk for a while and give her black looks and mutter under his breath about nursing vipers, but she'd give him a couple of very large whiskies and hope for the best.

'When do you intend calling on him?' she asked Dirk. 'He never gets back from Inverness till well after midnight. You'd better leave it till tomorrow.'

He thought that over for a moment, causing her to wonder if he'd changed his mind, then to her relief he nodded decisively. 'Right. Tomorrow morning. Tell him to expect me after breakfast.'

They indulged in one final, lingering kiss, then she pushed him away with gentle reluctance and a smile. 'You'll have to control those hands of yours. Until we're married, that is.'

She got out of the car then watched until he was out of sight. Only then did she brace herself and walk towards the house.

Morag was going to be the first hurdle. Her eyes never missed a thing, and true to form her first words were, 'Lord Almighty! I only washed and ironed that dress this morning. You look as if you fell into a peat bog. You'd better change and I'll wash it again.'

'It's all right, Morag. It's my own fault and I don't want to give you extra work. I'll do it myself.' She began pouring herself a cup of tea.

'You will not,' Morag retorted indignantly. 'You're
supposed to be the mistress of this house now. A fine
reflection it would be on me if folks heard that you
were doing your own washing! Anyway... how did
you get in such a mess? Where have you been all day?'

She took a deep breath. Morag could spot a lie at
fifty yards on a foggy night. 'Well, I may as well tell
you before you hear the gossip,' she said casually. 'I
spent the afternoon with Dirk MacAllister.'

The housekeeper looked at her in consternation.
'You didn't!'

'I did. He bought me lunch in the hotel then we
went in his boat to Para Mhor to look at a wreck.'

'But there was a terrible storm this afternoon.'

'It didn't start till we got there. When it did we took
shelter in the old croft.' And that was all she was going
to say on that subject, she thought grimly.

Morag cast an experienced eye at the stained and
creased dress then she pursed her lips and nodded.
'Aye... Well, I wouldn't tell your father, if I were
you. I don't think he'd be too pleased.'

After a long, hot soak in the bath she pulled on
jeans and a sweater before going down to the kitchen
to eat. It was going to be a long, nerve-racking evening
awaiting the confrontation with her father. Perhaps
it would have been better if that bolt of lightning
hadn't missed her after all.

The clock in the hall had just chimed ten and she
was curled up on the sofa in the library when Rory
came in.

Casting the book aside and getting to her feet, she
kissed him affectionately on the cheek then frowned
at his tired and worn appearance. 'You look as if you
need a drink. How was the auction?'

'A waste of time,' he said brusquely. 'I left early.'

He slumped into his armchair then accepted the large glass of whisky. 'Thanks, lass. Leave the bottle handy.' He took a large swallow, sighed and smacked his lips, then looked at her fondly. 'You're a bonny girl, Shona. I wish your mother had lived long enough to see how you've grown up. You've got my red hair, but when I look at your eyes it's like looking at her.' He sighed again, finished his glass, then held it out for a refill. 'Aye, you're about the only thing left in this world that means anything to me, Shona.'

Oh, God! she thought. Why did he have to be so maudlin tonight of all nights? How was she going to tell him now?

She turned her head away, afraid that he'd see the heart-sick expression on her face. She, his very own flesh and blood, was going to betray him. It might turn him against her forever. But there was no way out. She was trapped, both by her conscience and her promise to Dirk.

Swallowing the bitter bile in her throat, she said quietly, 'I . . . I've got something to tell you, Father. Something you may not like.'

His heavy brows came together, then he nodded at her to proceed. 'Go on, then. You've never been afraid to speak your mind before. It's too late to start changing the habits of a lifetime.'

She looked at him helplessly, then gathered her courage and said, 'Dirk MacAllister is calling to see you in the morning.'

He blinked once then growled, 'Is he indeed? And what have I done to deserve his company?'

She jerked the words out quickly. 'Dirk and I . . . We . . . we're getting married.'

There was a sharp crack as the glass splintered in his massive fist and he glared down at his hand and muttered, 'Damnation!'

His hand was badly cut and she rushed forward to help him, but he brushed her aside. Pulling a handkerchief from his pocket, he wrapped it tightly around the wound, then he turned his bleak eyes back to her. 'I'm going to pretend that I never heard that. No daughter of mine would ever lower herself enough to marry a MacAllister. Now get to bed and——'

A mixture of sorrow and defiance distorted her voice. 'Pretending won't do any good, Father. I'm going to marry him, and that's all there is to it.'

Colour suffused his face and there was a silence so taut that she could hear her heart thudding in her ears. She wanted to flee from the room and hide from the shocked anger in his eyes, but it was too late for that. Her only hope lay in calming him down and making him listen to reason.

'We...we're in love with each other, Father,' she declared in a voice that was still cracked and uneven.

'In love?' He repeated the words to himself like someone trying to understand a foreign language.

'Yes.' She added quickly, 'Dirk isn't at all like I'd been led to believe. He's not like his father. You can judge him for your——'

He cut her off savagely. 'How long have you been seeing him? Since you came back from university? Meeting with that cur behind my back! Lying and cheating! Deceiving me!'

The accusation first numbed her then provoked her to a stammering response. 'Th...that's not true. I...I haven't been lying to anyone. Or meeting Dirk in secret. I've never even spoken to him until this afternoon.'

'And on the basis of one afternoon's acquaintance you've decided to marry him?'

Even to her ears it sounded improbable and ridiculous. 'Yes . . . That's the truth, Father. I swear it. It . . . it all happened so suddenly. We just met and . . . and——'

Dark suspicion clouded his face and he thundered, 'Did you lie with him? Have you had carnal knowledge of each other?'

She winced. The biblical style and brutal manner of his interrogation made her feel like the whore of Babylon and she hung her head, waiting for his wrath to subside.

His breath rasped in his throat then he said heavily, 'Aye. I see you're not even bothering to deny it.' Shaking with rage, he drove the knife of his contempt deeper into her soul. 'If it had been with anyone else, I could have forgiven. But to allow yourself to be contaminated and defiled by a creature like that!'

'He isn't a creature,' she retorted, stung at last into a show of defiance. 'Just because you've always hated the MacAllisters——'

He made a gesture of damnatory dismissal and turned his back on her. 'Leave the room. This discussion is finished.'

Resentment flashed in her eyes. 'What discussion? You won't even listen to me, will you? Why should I have to suffer for your prejudices? The least you can do is agree to see him.'

He reached for his bottle and sneered, 'Aye. I'll see him. And when I do . . .' He left the threat unfinished and went to the cabinet for another glass.

The storm returned that night, no rain but a screeching, howling wind that made sleep next to impossible. In the darkness of her room she lay for hours tossing and turning and praying for oblivion and a release from the questions that haunted her mind.

Her father had ridiculed the idea that she could have fallen in love with Dirk after only such a brief encounter. Was he right? Was she simply confusing a strong sexual attraction for the real thing?

Dirk was the first man she'd ever completely submitted to. She recalled in every vivid detail the way he'd looked into her eyes and told her that he was going to make love to her. The thought of resisting him had never even entered her head. Her need for him had been sudden and overwhelming, a hunger that had ignored every constraint of decency and self-preservation in its craving for satisfaction. It had been self-indulgence on the grand scale.

The question that now disturbed her demanded an answer. In the same conditions could anyone other than Dirk have evoked the same feelings in her? The violence of the storm . . . the lightning that had almost killed her...then the warmth and intimacy of the fire. Then the way his experienced kisses and caresses had aroused her. All these things taken together had made her vulnerable. Was it possible that she might have surrendered as willingly to any other man?

No! She dared not allow herself to believe that. It had to be the real thing, because the price she was being asked to pay was too high for anything else. The love and respect of her father was something to be cherished and not thrown away lightly.

The hope that he'd have softened his attitude by morning was dashed when she went down to breakfast. Her polite greeting was met by a grim silence from across the table.

Morag, sensing the atmosphere, kept her chattering tongue still for once and made herself scarce as soon as the meal had been served.

Shona had little appetite, and the covert glances she chanced at the stony features opposite gave little comfort or hope for an understanding between them.

Finally he pulled his watch from his waistcoat pocket then lumbered to his feet and growled, 'If MacAllister dares to show his face around here tell him I'll be in the big shed loading the tractor.'

Her eyes pleaded with him. 'Can't you wait in the house for him, Father? I'm sure he'll be here shortly.'

His face darkened at the suggestion. 'You ask me to wait? Wait on him?' He roughly pushed his chair out of the way and stamped outside.

She bit her lip in agitation and glanced at the clock. She knew her father. It would take him no longer than half an hour to load the tractor and trailer, then he'd drive off into the hills somewhere and wouldn't return till late evening.

An agonising twenty minutes passed and she tried to keep herself busy in the library. For the last two weeks she had been trying to reorganise her father's bookkeeping methods into something more intelligible, but right now it was hard to concentrate.

Finally, in desperation, she found Dirk's number in the phone book and dialled his number. After an interminable wait the call was answered by his housekeeper.

'Hello. This is Shona Struan. Is Dirk there?'

'I'm afraid not, Miss Struan. Dirk has left.'

Thank God for that, she thought. 'Good. Then he must be on his way here.' She was about to hang up when the housekeeper spoke again.

'No, Miss Struan. I mean, he's gone.' She sounded bemused, as if she couldn't quite believe it herself. 'He packed a couple of suitcases and drove off about two hours ago. He said that he'd be making arrangements for a manager to run the place while he's gone.'

She replaced the phone with a frown, then stared at it. A feeling of cold dread began to steal over her. Something was wrong. Something was terribly, terribly wrong.

CHAPTER THREE

SHONA put down her empty cup and glanced at her watch in anger. This was getting ridiculous. She was being treated with deliberate contempt, and she wasn't going to stand for it.

'I'm sorry about this,' the housekeeper said in some embarrassment. 'Would you like more tea?'

'It's all right, Mrs Ross. I know it isn't your fault.'

'He has company. Some young lady from Edinburgh. Discussing business, I believe.'

More likely seducing her on the settee and taking his time about it, Shona thought savagely.

'How's Morag keeping? I haven't seen her since the party at the hotel last New Year.'

'She's fine, Mrs Ross. I'll tell her you were asking for her.'

'And Lachie? I saw young Jamie buying a new pair of jeans at the store last week. He's going to be as tall as his father by the looks of him.'

Shona knew that Mrs Ross was simply trying to lighten the tense atmosphere, and she had no wish to hurt the housekeeper's feelings, but her patience was nearing its limit.

'Look, Mrs Ross, would you mind going and asking him how much longer he intends keeping me hanging about? Tell him that my time is just as important as his and I've wasted enough of it already.'

Reluctantly Mrs Ross left the kitchen, leaving her to nurse her wrath and keep it warm. If there really was any truth in the rumour that he was going to build on Para Mhor she was going to fight him in the courts if necessary. Even if she didn't win she'd at least have had the satisfaction of holding up his plans and hopefully causing him expense. It might even be a good idea to round up some of her own hill sheep and transport them out to the island as they'd done in the old days. She'd only be exercising her right to common grazing, and it would certainly make things a lot more awkward for him. She'd talk the idea over with Lachie tomorrow.

'He'll see you now,' Mrs Ross announced a few minutes later when she returned to the kitchen. 'I'll take you to the library.'

She followed the housekeeper, her mind already rolling its sleeves up for the battle ahead and her face set with cold determination.

She'd only met him once in the last five years, and that had been when he'd turned up for Rory's funeral in the windswept churchyard. At the sight of him she'd dashed over to the Land Rover, grabbed the shotgun from the rack, and threatened him through a mist of rage and tears. She'd been in no condition to pay much attention to his appearance on that day, but she could see now that time hadn't changed him in the least. He was still lean and dark and dangerously attractive. And probably still as empty of substance, she thought witheringly.

He was standing in front of a huge log fire, hands clasped behind his back in typical lord-of-the-manor pose. A tall, willowy blonde by his side was regarding her with amiable curiosity.

Shona pointedly ignored her and snapped, 'This is a private matter, MacAllister. I'm sure you've no wish

to get your... friend... involved. Will you please ask
her to leave?'

The studied insult to his guest made Dirk stiffen
then he masked his displeasure behind a taut smile.
'Pamela would have gone by now, but when I told
her that you were an old friend of mine she expressed
a desire to meet you.'

'Yes...' murmured the blonde. Her brown eyes
studied Shona with barely hidden anger, then she be-
stowed a smile on Dirk. 'Well, I really must be going
now. Thanks for everything. I hope we can arrange
another meeting soon, Dirk.'

As she watched Dirk escorting his guest to the door
with his arm around her slim waist, she refused to
acknowledge the unaccountable feeling of resentment, and she turned away and glanced around
the room.

It was much as she'd imagined it would be, even
to the old oil-paintings of his ancestors on the walls.
The furniture was antique, everything from heavy
Jacobean to elegant Regency and ornate Victorian.
The smell was a pungent mixture of old leather, old
whisky and smouldering pine. Apart from the
standard lamps and the wall lights the room yielded
nothing to the dictates of modern fashion. It was too
smugly solid and respectable for comfort, she decided.

As soon as he'd closed the library door Dirk walked
over to a cabinet and called, 'What would you like
to drink?'

It was hard to keep the virulent animosity from her
voice. Her mission here had nothing to do with what
had happened in the past and she wasn't going to fall
into the trap of behaving like some hotheaded fool

seeking vengeance. That could wait for another time and place.

'Nothing,' she said coldly. 'I told you that this wasn't a social call.'

'Aye, so you did.' He poured a drink for himself then raised the glass mockingly. 'You weren't sociable to Pamela. In fact you were damnably rude and hostile.'

By sheer force of will she prevented herself from showing him just how rude and hostile she could be if she really tried. 'And you were a liar when you described me as an old friend,' she retaliated. 'You should have got rid of her before you asked me in. If you must flaunt your bimbo girlfriends in front of me don't expect me to shake their hands.'

'Still jumping to conclusions, I see.' He sounded like someone scolding a child for spilling their milk. 'Pamela isn't my girlfriend. She's a historical researcher from Edinburgh. We've got some documents and letters here about the Jacobite Rebellion, and she wanted to study them. And she isn't staying here. She has a room at the hotel.'

He took a sip of his drink, enjoying the flush of discomfort on her face, then he gave her another mocking smile. 'Don't feel too bad about it. I'll give her your apologies the next time I see her.'

She bit her lip in frustration and anger. No sooner had she stepped into the room than she'd made a fool of herself, and trust him to make the most of it.

She was still desperately thinking of some way to retrieve the initiative when he attacked her from another direction. 'It's quite remarkable how luscious you manage to look in an old sweater and jeans.' His insolent eyes savoured her in appreciation. 'Then again, it may just be that I remember the way you looked without any clothes.' He caught her wrist just in time and scolded her. 'Don't be naughty. You shouldn't try to slap someone who's just paid you a compliment.'

She wrenched her arm free and glared at him. 'Keep your damned compliments. I want nothing from you, MacAllister.'

One eyebrow rose in mocking scepticism. 'That's hard to believe. You must want something. You said this wasn't a social call.' His eyebrow came down sharply. 'Perhaps at long last you want to apologise for the way you behaved at your father's funeral.'

'You're lucky I didn't pull the trigger,' she fumed.

'And you're lucky I didn't put you over my knee and give you a damned good hiding.' His eyes became hard and bitter. 'But that would have embarrassed you in front of the crowd, and I couldn't do that, could I? Not at your own father's funeral. So I allowed you to go ahead and humiliate me instead.'

'You deserved it,' she flung at him. 'You deserved worse for the way you treated and humiliated me.'

The bitterness faded from his grey eyes, leaving them curiously flat and empty, and he shrugged. 'Then we're even.'

Even . . . ? She almost laughed outright in his face.

'It was five years ago,' he went on quietly. 'Are you going to call a truce or are you going to carry on denying yourself the one thing you want?'

She frowned at him. 'And what would that be?'

'A man to take you in his arms. A man who'll love and protect you.'

The man was incredible, she thought. Totally and utterly incredible! Did he really think she was going to fall for that? Did he think she had a sponge for a brain? Well, there was one way to find out.

Summoning up the last ounce of her self-control, she adopted a thoughtful, contrite expression and murmured, 'Five years is a terribly long time, I suppose. And I dare say you must have had good reason for... for leaving suddenly, the way you did.' She paused and gave a reluctant yet understanding smile. 'Thank God I wasn't pregnant after all, and that's something to be grateful for. But if I had been I'm sure you'd have made adequate provision for your child.'

'Of course. That goes without saying.'

It was almost more than she could stomach to go on with this charade, but she nodded. 'It's all water under the bridge now, isn't it? We really should make an attempt to forget and forgive. There's no reason we can't at least be friends, bury the hatchet at last. Right?'

He studied her in narrow-eyed silence for a moment, then he permitted himself the faintest of smiles. 'I'm glad to see you're taking a reasonable attitude at last. What happened was unfortunate, but I had no——'

This time she was too quick for him and there was a loud, painful-sounding crack as her hand lashed across his cheek. 'You lying, two-faced, contemptible piece of garbage,' she spat. 'The only place I want to bury a hatchet is in your black, cowardly heart.' Hot tears came to her eyes and she launched another attack, this time pummelling her fists against his chest. 'You're a despicable excuse for a man. You're nothing but a——' She gasped as he grabbed her and pulled her violently close to him.

'Stop it' he barked harshly. 'You're getting hysterical, you little fool.'

She clenched her teeth. 'Let me go, you pig.'

'Not until you've calmed down.'

It was getting hard to breathe now, the way he was crushing her. 'All right . . .' she gasped. 'You're bigger and stronger than I am. You don't have to prove it.'

He let her go and she stood glaring at him as he walked back to the drinks cabinet. He returned with a glass of neat whisky and thrust it at her. 'Drink this.'

'Keep your bloody drink,' she grated. 'I don't want it.'

'Take the damned thing and try to calm down,' he growled.

She knocked the glass from his hand. 'I don't want to calm down. I'm enjoying every minute of this. I've waited a long time to tell you how much I detest you.'

He stared down at the shattered glass and the spreading stain on the carpet, then he looked up and said icily, 'Well, since you're enjoying yourself so much I see no reason why I should miss out on the fun.'

This was turning out all wrong, she thought with dismay. She hadn't come here to rake over the past. He'd been the one to resurrect it, but she should have ignored the bait and brushed it aside with silent contempt. Cold indifference could sometimes be a more subtle and painful weapon than hot-blooded anger. But then it was her father's blood that ran in her veins, and the Struans had always been open and honest about their feelings. They'd never gone in for deceit, and because of that she'd fallen into the very trap she'd intended to avoid.

His remark about not missing out on the fun didn't make sense to her until an instant later when she found herself imprisoned in his steel-sinewed arms once more.

Her eyes widened in surprise. 'What do you think you're doing? Let me go.'

'You don't really mean that, Shona. This is why you really came, isn't it?' His voice sounded dangerously laden with desire, and she gulped. He went on taunting her. 'It's only your stupid Struan pride that has kept you away so long. All that time your body has been aching for mine. We both walked in heaven that day on Para Mhor, and you've been yearning to get back there ever since. And you know you'll never reach it without me. We were born for each other. You feel it as much as I do.'

'Let me go,' she mouthed. 'You...you're having a brainstorm. The only thing I feel for you is contempt.'

He smiled thinly. 'I don't think so, Shona.'

'That's because you're a conceited oaf. Any good feelings I had about you disappeared long ago.'

He smiled coldly. 'So you say. But we'll try a little experiment, shall we? Let's find out the truth.' His mouth dropped on hers, and in desperation she sought to break the contact by twisting her head from side to side, but it only succeeded in making her breathless.

When he finally took his mouth from hers she drew in a lungful of air then spluttered and gasped in outrage, 'You...you were hurting me. Let me go, damn you.'

'No,' he said thoughtfully. 'I think you enjoyed being hurt. I think you'd prefer it if I took you by force, because then you wouldn't have to admit that you'd lusted after a hated MacAllister. You'd have the sexual pleasure without having to feel guilty about it.'

He was serious! She could tell by that look in his eyes. He really believed what he was saying! 'No!' she gasped again. 'You're wrong. I don't want you to touch me. Please, Dirk...'

His eyes and predatory smile mocked her. 'Scream as loud as you like if it makes you feel any better. You can act the part of the outraged maiden to your heart's content. Scream abuse at me. Plead. Cry and sob. It'll ease your conscience and make my own pleasure in taking you all the sweeter.'

Before her numbed mind had time to react he removed her loose-fitting sweater by simply pulling it up from the bottom and yanking it roughly over her head. An instant later her bra was ripped off and tossed aside.

White-faced by now with shock and apprehension, she vainly tried to hide her near nakedness as she backed away from him, but he was too quick, and once more she found herself imprisoned in his arms. His right hand came up to caress her breast, and at the instant, swelling response he whispered in her ear, 'You see what I mean, Shona? Your tongue tells me one thing, but your body says another. You want me, don't you?'

The sensual touch of his fingers turned her protest into a trembling moan that bubbled up through the constriction in her throat and escaped her lips. Her mind rebelled at her weakness, but forces older and stronger than the rules of civilised behaviour were demolishing her defences and wrecking her will-power.

Dark and shameful excitement rampaged through her veins and turned her limbs to jelly.

Sensing her willingness to capitulate, he challenged her, 'Not yet, surely? What's wrong with my little red-haired tigress? Aren't you going to fight? What about the scratching and kicking? There's no fun for me in this. You're not going to spoil the occasion for me, are you? Have you forgotten that I'm a MacAllister? We've been sworn enemies for generations.'

The flint edge of his sarcasm sparked a tiny flame of cold sanity, and she raised her hands against his shirt front and summoned enough strength to push. Her puny effort filled him with amusement and he taunted her, 'Come on, Shona. You can do better than that. You should be defending your honour with tooth and claw.'

She was suddenly aware of something giving, and she realised with a mounting horror and desperation that he'd unzipped her jeans.

'Well, perhaps not,' he conceded with a cold smile. 'Some things are stronger than a sense of honour, aren't they? Hunger, for example. Hunger for loving and the feel of a man. Let's find out how hungry you are, shall we?'

In desperation she clung to the waistband of her jeans and succeeded at last in wriggling free from his grasp. She put her hand out in front of her defensively and wavered, 'No, Dirk. Please...that's enough.'

He stood for a moment surveying her, then he gave a laugh that scraped at her nerve-endings. 'All right. Relax. I'm not going to hurt you, but I think I proved my point. Wouldn't you say so?'

He picked her clothes up from the floor and handed them to her, then said gruffly, 'Cover yourself up before I change my mind.'

She pulled up her zip, then, ignoring the torn bra, she hastily donned her sweater. The only thing to cover now was her embarrassment, and she hid that behind a deluge of indignation. 'You should be locked up. The only thing you've proved is that you're no gentleman. I don't know why I should be surprised, though. I found that out a long time ago, didn't I?'

He went over to the cabinet again. 'Are you sure you wouldn't like that drink now?' he asked affably. 'It's a very fine twelve-year-old malt. Not yet on the market. I'd like your opinion.'

'You know what you can do with your drink,' she fumed.

'Tut, tut. You're certainly proving that you're no lady.' He filled his glass, then turned and raised it mockingly. 'However, I'm sure that given a little time and co-operation on your part we can knock the rough edges off and make you presentable enough for decent society. You've been on your own for far too long.'

Her blue eyes blazed at him and she snapped, 'You just love making a fool of me, don't you? It must give you a tremendous kick, considering the lengths you go to.'

He sipped his drink thoughtfully, then laid down the glass and began lecturing her. 'My dear young lady——'

'I'm not your "dear young lady",' she grated. 'I'm not your "dear young" anything.'

He shrugged. 'Very well. Miss Struan, I had no intention of making a fool of you. I merely wanted to satisfy my curiosity. Was your body still as beautiful as ever and was it as easily aroused by my touch? I'm glad to see that it is on both counts.'

She clenched her fists in frustration. 'You're despicable.'

'You've already said that.' His voice was deceptively mild and at odds with the hard glint of anger in his eyes. 'You've developed quite a vocabulary, but I'd be obliged if you'd practise it on someone else. I might forget I'm a gentleman after all and decide to finish what I started to teach you a lesson.'

'Just try it and see what happens,' she warned darkly.

He laughed at her look of belligerence, then continued drily, 'The last time I saw you you threatened to do unspeakable things to me with a shotgun. I see you haven't mellowed with age.'

'You're right. I haven't.'

'But you can't deny you feel a certain…excitement when we're together?'

'I'm not even going to bother answering that,' she said stiffly.

A smile lurked at the back of his eyes, and as they weighed her in silence she felt herself colouring. He couldn't possibly be right, could he? Was her soul, her subconscious mind, still yearning for him? Oh, no, God! Please let that not be true. But if it was? He seemed to be convinced of it. According to him he'd just proved it.

What kind of malevolent sorcery had cast its spell over her? How could she have been so out of touch with reality? After the way he'd treated her you'd have thought that she'd have had more self-control, instead of behaving like some brainless moth bent on self-destruction in a candle-flame.

Why did he affect her in such a way? What was it about him? He was like some elemental force without a conscience. She'd barely been in the room five minutes before he'd begun ripping her clothes off, and now he was acting as if nothing had happened!

His eyes were still weighing and dissecting her, and she flushed. 'Stop staring at me like that.'

'Like what?' he asked innocently.

'Like a fox at a chicken,' she retorted.

His dark features arranged themselves into something resembling a pleasant smile. 'I can't help it. Anyway, let's get down to business. Now as I see it——'

'I'm not the least bit interested in how you see anything,' she informed him in an icy voice. 'My business here is about Para Mhor.'

'Para Mhor?' He gave a sigh of reminiscence. 'So I was right. You just can't forget that wonderful day either.'

She ignored the suggestion, gritted her teeth, and said, 'I hear that you intend building on it.'

'Is that so?'

She waited for him to go on, but he didn't. 'Well?' she demanded. 'Are you going to deny it?'

He shrugged. 'Whether I intend to or not isn't any of your business as far as I can see. Why should you worry?'

'Para Mhor has always been common grazing,' she reminded him sharply. 'If you are going to build there you'll have to ask my permission.'

'And would you give it?'

'Never as long as I live,' she told him with quiet satisfaction. 'Never.'

'Why? Do you intend putting sheep on the island?' he asked mildly.

'I might. Then again I might not. That isn't the point,' she said tartly.

'No?' He looked puzzled. 'Then what is the point?'

She glared at him. 'You never asked me first. That's the point.'

He nodded to himself. 'I see. So you're just being bloody-minded. What if I told you that I wanted to build a holiday home for orphans?'

She looked at him in confusion. 'Well, in that case ... I ... I ...'

His mouth quirked in derision. 'All right. Don't get your moral principles in a twist. I don't intend doing anything on Para Mhor.'

'Lachie heard that you'd had a surveyor out there,' she challenged. 'Something about chalets and a marina.'

He waved a hand in a lazy gesture of dismissal. 'What Lachie heard was rumour. You should pay no attention to rumours.'

'You mean it's not true?'

'Not a word of it.'

She narrowed her eyes at him doubtfully. 'I don't know whether to believe you or not, MacAllister. You're such a smooth-talking, devious liar I wouldn't trust you with the pennies on a dead man's eyes.'

A threatening shadow crossed his face and he growled, 'Watch your tongue, woman. I can excuse insults made in the heat of the moment, but not that.'

She bit her lip in frustration. If he really was telling the truth, then that meant that she need never have come here and suffered all this aggravation. She didn't know whether to feel merely angry or downright furious.

She stiffened as she saw his eyes mock her again, then he drawled, 'The truth is that it was I who deliberately started the rumour. I knew that you'd get to hear of it sooner or later and that when you did you'd act in typical Struan style and come charging out here spitting fire and fury.' He paused then gave a crooked smile. 'Mind you, I didn't expect you to arrive at night in the middle of a storm. I didn't realise that you were that impetuous.'

As his words sunk in her resentment flared up. 'Is this your idea of some sadistic joke?'

'You're to blame,' he told her easily. 'You've refused to see me or have anything to do with me since I came back. I had to find some way of meeting you so that we could talk things over.'

The realisation of how easily she'd been tricked and manipulated gave her a sick, empty feeling. What a fool she'd been! And just look at him sitting there with that smug smile on his face!

'All right,' she said truculently. 'Your childish trick worked and I fell for it. That probably gives your ego something to crow about, but it was all a waste of time. I can't think of a single thing I want to talk over with you.'

'Not even the fact that you're going broke and may have to sell up?' he asked softly.

At the sudden harsh reminder of her real problem a hard knot settled in her stomach and she muttered, 'You shouldn't believe every little rumour you hear either.'

'It's no rumour. I'm talking hard facts.' He began reciting them in the cold, impersonal manner of a bank manager advising a client that he couldn't afford a mortgage. 'You don't have to be a genius to work it out. Eighty per cent of your income comes from organised shooting parties. For the last two seasons those six hunting lodges your father built in Glen Gallan have lain empty. The new season begins in about three months and you still haven't got a booking.'

'They'll come,' she muttered with more hope than certainty.

He shook his head at the dim prospect. 'Even if they do you'll have to be booked solid for the next four years before you get back on your feet.'

The fact that his assessment of the situation was pretty near the mark only increased the resentment she felt at his intrusion into her private affairs.

'I fail to see how it can be of any concern to you,' she said stiffly.

'It is if you decide to sell to an outsider, Shona. I can't allow that to happen.'

She raised her eyebrows at him. 'Oh, can't you? If I do have to sell I'll sell to anyone I please. But one thing you can be sure of, it won't be you.'

It was obviously no more than he expected, and he shook his head at her obstinacy. 'Aye. It's not that my money is different from anyone else's. You just can't stomach the idea of a MacAllister owning your land. That's it, isn't it?'

'I couldn't have put it better myself,' she mocked. 'Now I think that's all to be said on the subject, so I'll take my leave.'

'Not so fast.' He had her tightly by the arm again.

She already knew the futility of trying to escape once he had a grip on her, and she stood with a look of impatience on her face. 'Don't waste your time or mine,' she advised him caustically. 'As long as I'm alive you'll never get your hands on Struan property.'

'Don't be too sure about that,' he growled. 'I could make you bankrupt within a month if I wanted to. If your estate is put into the hands of liquidators they're duty bound to accept the highest offer, and I'll make sure that offer is mine.'

Her eyes searched his face in the hope that he was bluffing, but the only thing she saw was steel-hard determination. No, Dirk MacAllister wasn't the type to make empty threats. He'd probably bought some of her debts at a discount. That way he could demand payment from her any time he wanted.

Bitterness welled up in her throat. What would happen to Morag and Lachie and Jamie and the other tenants who depended on her?

'Haven't you got enough?' she asked him with contempt. 'Is it just greed that drives you, or are you still trying to settle old scores between our families?'

'Neither,' he snapped in anger. 'I'm not interested in acquiring Struan land.' For a moment his eyes held the cold, calculating glitter of a hunter with his quarry in his sights, then he gave a sardonic twist to his lips. 'There is one thing I'm very keen on acquiring, though. You.'

She was instantly on her guard and she warned him grimly, 'If you start mauling me about again I'll——'

'I'm talking about marriage,' he said impatiently.

She didn't know whether to break into hysterical laughter or hit him with something extremely heavy. Taking a deep breath and eyeing him belligerently, she said, 'Will you let go of my arm? My bloody fingers are going numb.'

'Not until you've given me your answer.'

Exasperation put a saw edge to her voice. 'You must take me for a complete idiot.'

'You will be if you refuse my offer. Once you become my wife there will be no question of your having to sell out to anyone.' His grip strengthened and he drew her remorselessly closer until their lips were almost touching. 'But the main reason is that you want me just as much as I want you. You and I, we set each other alight, Shona.'

She shook her head, knowing that if she tried to speak her voice would betray her sudden feeling of weakness.

His left hand slid under her sweater and gently caressed the bare flesh of her back. 'Do you want me to prove it again?' he asked in a hoarse whisper. 'I'll willingly spend the rest of the night doing just that.'

This was absolute madness, she thought. Why was her heart hammering so wildly? She knew the kind of man he was, so why couldn't her stupid body behave itself?

'We could have been married five years ago,' she reminded him bitterly. 'But you were scared to face up to my father. You left me with egg all over my face. You ... you didn't even write. No explanation. No sorry. Nothing. How could I marry a man who'd done a thing like that to me?'

'I had to leave. Something unforeseen came up and I had no option.'

She studied his face for a sign. Any sign. It was nothing but a mask of cold granite. He had spoken, and she was expected to accept it and be grateful.

'I'm sorry, Dirk. That just isn't good enough.'

'It's all you're getting for now,' he said unequivocally. 'But if it's any consolation to you I can tell you that the last five years without you have been bleak and empty and not worth a damn.' Abruptly he released her, as if suddenly distancing himself from what he was about to say. 'Either you agree to marry me, Shona, or I'll have to destroy you and take your land. It's as simple as that. Now you'd better go home and think about it.'

'I don't have to think about it,' she said with quiet dignity. 'You almost destroyed me once, but I survived. I dare say I can do it again.' Turning her back on him, she left the room quickly before he had a chance to see the tears of anger and frustration that were beginning to glisten in her eyes.

CHAPTER FOUR

THE weather had worsened while Shona and
MacAllister had been at each other's throats, and as
she drove home her knuckles were white on the
steering-wheel. On the exposed heights of the moor
above Kinvaig the force of the wind tore off the
nearside windscreen wiper, and even the noise of the
jeep's labouring engine was lost in the black howling
of the storm. Ahead of her the unmarked and un-
fenced road was barely visible as the headlights reflected back from the torrential rain.

She'd only gone about three miles when the engine
misfired, jerked, then misfired again and cut out. Blast
it! Perhaps the rain had got into the ignition. She tried
the key, but nothing happened apart from the headlights dimming as the battery power was diverted to
the starter motor. Petrol? She looked at the gauge,
then groaned in disgust. Empty! What an idiot she
was. Why hadn't she checked before she'd left?

Wishing there were something handy she could
strangle with her bare hands, she switched off the
headlights to conserve power and peered through the
blurred windscreen. One thing was for certain: there
wouldn't be anyone else using this road on a night
like this. No one else was as stupid as she was.

She felt under the dash for the microphone
of the CB radio and switched it on. 'Lachie...
Morag... Anyone...?'

There were three CB sets back on the estate. Lachie had one in his Land Rover and one in his lodge. The third one was in Morag's kitchen. More than once they'd proved their worth when no phones were handy, and she prayed that this time would be no exception.

She waited for an answer. Thirty seconds passed, then she tried again.

Suddenly Morag's voice came tinnily from the speaker. 'Aye? Is that you, Shona?'

'Is Lachie there?'

Lachie's rasping voice came on a moment later. 'What's wrong?'

'I've run out of petrol. About a mile south of Kinvaig.' She could just imagine what Lachie was saying to himself.

'OK. I'll phone old Stewart at Kinvaig garage. He'll bring you a couple of gallons in the van.'

'No,' she said quickly. 'The garage will be closed for the night. I ... I'd rather not bother him.' She paused, wondering if a feeling of embarrassment could be detected over a radio. 'I'd rather you came in the Land Rover and towed me home.'

There was a grunt from the speaker, then, 'Aye ... Have it your own way, then. I'll be there in about fifteen minutes.'

She switched off and replaced the microphone, then sat drumming her fingers on the steering-wheel in frustration. She still hadn't settled last month's fuel bill at the garage, nor the month's before that. When you already owed someone as much money as she did to Stewart you didn't ask him to leave a warm fireside on a night like this just to deliver a couple of gallons of petrol which you were going to have to add to the bill in any case. It was better to keep a low profile, even though she knew that Stewart was a reasonable man. He realised that everyone was going through a bad patch at the moment. But things were bound to pick up. However, everyone wasn't as patient as Stewart. It was the vultures you had to be wary of. Vultures like MacAllister, ready to swoop and pick over the bones.

She reflected bitterly on his 'proposal', if it could be called such. Just for a moment back then she'd almost believed him, had wanted desperately to believe him, but his refusal to offer any explanation about deserting her and his arrogant take-it-or-leave-it attitude had brought her to earth with a sickening thud.

No. It wasn't a wife he was wanting. Marrying her would simply be the easiest and cheapest way for him to get his hands on her property. No matter how he dressed it up with fancy emotional words about setting each other alight or how his life had been bleak and empty without her for the last five years, his only motive was greed. The MacAllisters had always been infamous for coveting other people's possessions. It was in their blood, and he was merely carrying on the family tradition.

Her thoughts remained dark and bitter until with relief she saw the headlights of the Land Rover coming to her rescue.

Half an hour later she was in the warmth of her own kitchen, drying off in front of the Aga. The fawn rose awkwardly from the corner and came over to nudge her legs in greeting. Distracted with her own problems, she stroked it absent-mindedly.

'Well?' asked Morag.

She frowned at the housekeeper. 'Well what?'

Morag banged the lid down impatiently on the teapot. 'Did you find out what he's building on Para Mhor? That's why you went to see him, wasn't it?'

'It was only a rumour. He isn't interested in Para Mhor.'

It wasn't good enough for Morag, and she muttered sourly, 'Well, you must have spoken about something. You were gone long enough.'

Shona whirled on her angrily. 'It's none of your damn business what we talked about. Now just get on with what you're doing and leave me in peace.'

Morag stiffened as if she'd received a bucket of icy water in the face.

Instantly Shona was overwhelmed by a feeling of shame, and she hurried forward and hugged the housekeeper. 'Oh, my God, Morag! I didn't mean to say that. Please forgive me.'

The shocked resentment slowly faded from the housekeeper's eyes and she said primly, 'Aye... Well, I can see you're upset right enough. But you're right. It's none of my business. I'm just the housekeeper around here. From now on I'll stick to cooking and cleaning.'

The sarcastic rebuke made Shona wince, more so because she knew she thoroughly deserved it, and she said miserably, 'I've had a terrible night and I'm still on edge. But I realise that's no excuse, Morag. I'm just a selfish fool.'

'Humph! Well, I wouldn't call you selfish. As for being a fool, you're no worse than your father was.' She led Shona towards the table, made her sit down, then stood over her with folded arms. 'Perhaps you've forgotten, but I'm the one you used to come to sobbing when you fell and hurt yourself, or when your doll's head fell off, or when you fell into the burn and got soaked and were afraid your father would find out. Well, it looks to me like you're in trouble again, but this time you're too high and mighty to come to me. You don't need me any more. You don't need anyone any more. You're too proud and independent for that. Am I right?'

She stood in silence, contemplating Shona's expression of abject misery, then she snorted. 'Aye. It's just as I thought.' She poured two cups of tea, laid one in front of Shona, then sat down beside her and said quietly, 'Tell me what's wrong. Maybe we can put your doll's head back on.'

Shona felt a surge of affection for the older woman. There was no way that Morag could help her with this crisis, but at least it might help to have a sympathetic ear to pour her troubles into. She lifted her cup, warming her hands on it, then said, 'I suppose you must have guessed that I'm having money troubles. Everything going out and very little coming in.'

Morag nodded. 'Aye. Lachie and me aren't stupid, you know. We've talked it over. We've both got a bit saved for our retirement. It's yours if you need it.'

A lump arose in Shona's throat. 'I . . . I couldn't let you do that.'

Morag shrugged. 'It's our own money. We can do what we like with it. You can pay us back when you get on your feet.'

Shona felt humbled by their loyalty and devotion. 'What if I don't manage to get back on my feet?' she asked quietly. 'What if I have to sell the estate?'

It was a possibility that obviously hadn't occurred to Morag, and her features hardened. 'Is it as bad as that, then?'

Shona nodded. 'I'm afraid it is. In fact it's even worse. I may end up having to sell to Dirk MacAllister. Would you be willing to work for him?'

'MacAllister!' Morag stared at her in amazement. 'You wouldn't let him get his hands on this place, surely?'

'He doesn't want me to sell out to anyone else,' Shona explained patiently. 'He's got my back to the wall, Morag. I've already had an offer from his lawyer. It would be more than enough to keep us all fairly comfortable for the rest of our lives. If I refuse his offer and look for another buyer he'll force me into bankruptcy and get his hands on the place that way.'

'He told you all this himself? To your face?'

Shona laid her cup down and got to her feet, suddenly too wound up with indignation to sit still. 'He did. And he enjoyed every minute of it. But you haven't heard the best part yet. The cretin had the effrontery to ask me to marry him. It would solve all my problems, he said.' She made a sound of derision. 'Can you imagine me changing my name to Mrs MacAllister?'

Morag stared up at her in thoughtful silence for a moment, then shrugged. 'That might not be such a bad idea. You could do a lot worse.'

'What?' Her eyes widened at the shock of this stab in the back. 'Are you serious?'

'Why not?' asked Morag, unperturbed by her reaction.

She spread her arms in a mute appeal to Heaven, then unleashed a volley. 'I can't believe I'm hearing this! Why not? Because he's Dirk MacAllister, that's why not.'

'That doesn't seem like much of a reason to me,' Morag said drily.

Shona ground her teeth. 'All right, then. I'll give you a reason. I won't marry him because he's a greedy, lying, two-faced rat.'

'Not according to Mrs Ross, his housekeeper,' Morag said with infuriating calmness. 'She thinks the world of him. He's a real gentleman, she says, kind and considerate.'

'I don't give a damn what Mrs Ross says.'

'Well, you should. After all, she's known him since he was a child. How long have you known him?'

'Long enough,' grated Shona.

'I doubt it,' Morag said mildly. 'Apart from tonight, how many times have you met and spoken to the man?'

She was perplexed and annoyed at Morag's attitude and she complained wryly, 'You sound as if you're on his side. I'd expected a bit of sympathy from you at least.'

'Of course I'm on your side,' Morag said testily. 'But I thought it was advice you were wanting. I've never heard of a Struan asking for sympathy from anyone.'

'I see,' Shona said bitterly. 'So that's your advice, is it? Just throw in the towel and give in to his threats? Marry him and hand over my estate without a fight?'

'Well, that's what I'd do if a man loved me as much as he seems to love you.'

'Love!' exclaimed Shona. 'He doesn't love me. The only thing he loves is wealth and power.'

'Then why is he offering you half of everything he owns? If he's as greedy as you say he is, why would he want to share it with you?'

That side of the argument caught Shona by surprise, and she blinked as the sharp edge of her anger became blurred in a sudden fog of confusion. MacAllister offering all that on a plate? No. She couldn't believe that for one minute. His motive had to be something dark and underhand that she hadn't yet thought about.

Sensing her confusion, Morag continued to demolish her objections. 'You didn't think about that, did you? His estate is about four times the size of this place, not counting all the other interests he has. As his wife you'll be entitled to half of everything. He's the one with something to lose, not you. So that leaves only one other possibility. The man must truly be in love with you, whether you like it or not.'

Try as she might, she could find no way to refute the cold logic behind Morag's assertion. But Morag didn't know all the facts. Perhaps it was time she did.

'You're wrong, Morag,' she said quietly. 'I know you're wrong about him loving me, because he promised to marry me once before. He swore that he loved me, and I was stupid enough to believe him. But he didn't. He let me down.'

Morag didn't seem the least bit surprised. Instead she gave a wise, sympathetic nod. 'Aye. I guessed as much a long time ago.'

'You guessed!' She looked at the housekeeper in frank disbelief. 'Rubbish! Impossible! The only one who knew was my father, and he certainly never told anyone.'

A smile, half pitying and half amused, greeted her emotional outburst. 'I might be old, but I'm far from senile yet. I've got eyes and a long memory and I'm still able to put two and two together.'

Shona kept a discreet and chastened silence. This had already been a night of shocking surprises, and by the looks of it there were more to come.

Morag began to reminisce with an air of quiet satisfaction. 'I remember the day you came home and told me that Dirk had taken you to Para Mhor. There'd been a terrible storm and you'd both taken shelter in the old croft. But by the looks of your clothes and the state you were in I knew you'd been doing more than just holding hands. Aye...and the very next morning Dirk packed his bags and went down south.' She paused then added reflectively, 'As if that wasn't suspicious enough you were like an angry wildcat for the next two weeks, spitting and hissing at everyone in reach.'

Shona listened to Morag with deepening dismay. If Morag had guessed the truth how many others must have done so? Another memory rose like a gibbering spectre to haunt her—the memory of her and Dirk arriving in Kinvaig and the speculative looks her dishevelled appearance had drawn from the idlers on the pier. In her innocence and happiness at the time she hadn't given a fig what people thought. But by the following day, when Dirk had gone, had they, like Morag, begun to put two and two together...? The thought made Shona squirm. Had she been the laughing-stock of the Western Highlands for all these years, an object of ridicule with people pointing the finger and laughing behind her back?

Hanging on to the last shreds of her dignity, she admitted angrily, 'All right, dammit! I let Dirk MacAllister make love to me that day on Para Mhor. He asked me to marry him and I said yes. Then he promised to come to the house the following morning to talk to my father, but he didn't turn up. I never saw him again until the day of Rory's funeral.'

Morag eyed her sharply. 'You said that your father knew about it. Did you confess all this to him?'

The question raised Shona's hackles even further and she snapped, 'I wouldn't have been much of a daughter if I hadn't, would I? Of course I told him— that very night when he got back from Inverness.'

'Oh, aye? And what did he have to say about it?'

She bit her lip. 'What do you think? He wasn't exactly overjoyed.'

Even after all these years she could still recall in vivid detail the way his glass had splintered in his hand when she'd broken the news to him.

Morag nodded. 'Aye. I can imagine. But you never ever thought to confide in me, did you? All this time and not one word about it until now. I had to wonder and guess at the truth for myself.'

Guilt spread a flush over her face and she lowered her eyes. 'I . . . I'm sorry, Morag. When MacAllister left me in the lurch I felt nothing but shame. To have let myself be used by any man was bad enough. But a MacAllister! After all the warnings I'd had! I . . . I just wanted to forget the whole thing. But now he's back and you're telling me to go ahead and marry him as if nothing had ever happened.'

The sigh that emanated from Morag's lips could have signified either exasperation or indifference, but Shona couldn't decide which. All she was aware of was that an old wound had been ripped open and once again MacAllister was going to torment her like a fever in the night.

'Dirk might have had to leave because of pressing family business,' Morag said drily. 'You could at least give him the benefit of the doubt, but I suppose that's too much to ask for.'

'Aye. You're damn right it is,' she replied heatedly. 'He didn't even take the bother to write.'

Morag sighed again. 'So you're more interested in taking revenge on him than accepting his proposal?'

'Well, I hadn't thought about it,' she said grimly. 'But now you mention it it wouldn't be such a bad idea.'

Morag got stiffly to her feet and painfully straightened her back. 'Hmphh. That should come natural to you, then. The Struans were always good at the subject of revenge. Masters of the craft, you might say. Your father was the best of all, and if he was alive now he'd be telling you to marry Dirk and make the poor wretch's life so miserable that he'd be begging you for a divorce after six months. Then you'd end up with half of everything he owns, and that would teach him not to mess about with the Struans, wouldn't it?' She paused then added sourly, 'Aye. That would give the sly old devil something to chuckle about in his grave.'

That final, disparaging remark offended Shona and she frowned in annoyance. 'What do you mean—"sly old devil"?'

'Nothing.'

'You must have meant something by it,' she demanded.

Morag refused to meet her eyes and muttered, 'I'll not be speaking ill of the dead. Now, if you've finished with the tea I'd like to get to my bed.'

The housekeeper's uncalled-for remark still rankled in her mind as she tried in vain to get some sleep that night. There had been nothing 'sly' about Rory. He'd never done anything behind anyone's back. His reputation for direct and violent action against anyone who had the audacity to challenge him had been a local legend. It had certainly been enough to scare off Dirk MacAllister when it came to the crunch. In spite of his airy, arrogant promises of the day before he must have lain awake that night in a blue funk at the thought of confronting Rory in the morning, and in the end he'd scampered off with his tail between his legs.

She could still recall the cold contempt in her father's voice when he'd learnt that Dirk had sneaked off rather than face up to him. Not just contempt for Dirk, but contempt for her for having had anything to do with him in the first place.

'And that's the kind of worm you'd intended marrying, is it?' he'd asked sneeringly. 'Haven't I told you often enough the treacherous kind of scum they are? Have you forgotten Glen Gallan...the women and children massacred by the English redcoats while the MacAllisters stood by cheering? Did you not think of the shame you were bringing to the House of Struan by allowing the likes of him to violate you?'

He'd never referred to it ever again after that, but she could tell how deeply he'd been affected by her disregard for family pride and honour. No matter how hard she'd tried to make it up to him he'd become more withdrawn as time had passed, treating her more like a stranger not to be trusted than a daughter.

But it had been his physical decline that had caused her real worry. Always a man of immense strength and endurance, his steps had become slower, his shoulders more stooped, and the fire in his eyes had become dimmer. Her concern for his health had eventually reached the point when she'd demanded that he should see a doctor, but, as if to emphasise the rift that had grown between them, he'd completely ignored her pleas.

Then one night he'd locked himself in the library. In the morning they'd had to get Lachie to break the door down, and they'd found him slumped in his favourite armchair, his face as grey and cold as the ashes in the fireplace.

Rory's heart had finally given out, Dr Munroe had told her later that day, but she alone knew the truth. His heart would have been all right if she hadn't broken it in the first place, and no amount of tears would ever wash the guilt from her soul.

Perhaps Morag was right after all, she thought now as she lay staring into the darkness of her room. If Dirk MacAllister had caused her to break her father's heart it was only fitting that for the sake of vengeance she should now break his, marry him and make his life a living hell. It was a sweet thought, but she wondered if she'd ever have the stomach to go through with it.

CHAPTER FIVE

THE weather took a dramatic change for the better over the next few days, and by the Friday, when the ground had dried sufficiently, Shona set off with Lachie in the Land Rover to check over the shooting lodges in Glen Gallan.

They'd lain empty and shuttered since the previous October, and it was now time to air them and check for any winter damage that might need to be repaired before the start of the new season. That was providing they were lucky enough to receive any bookings, of course. The way things were going it was unlikely, but they still had to be prepared.

During the Second World War Glen Gallan had been chosen for its remoteness by the Army as a commando training base, and it was they who had built the road over which they were now travelling. Adequate in its day, it had now deteriorated to such an extent that it was going to cost a small fortune just to reinstate it to a reasonable standard. Lachie drove slowly, managing to avoid the worst of the pot-holes, but by the time they reached the lip of the glen she felt that every bone in her body had been shaken loose.

They both got out of the Land Rover to stretch their legs, and as she looked down into the glen below she felt, as she always did, that it was the most beautiful place on earth. The whole of the Western Highlands possessed a magical beauty of its own, but Glen Gallan was the jewel in the crown. Scooped out of the hard granite by the advancing glaciers of the Ice Age, it was now a long, narrow valley of emerald-green flanked by blue and purple heather-covered slopes.

In the old days it had been the ideal place for hiding cattle from the marauding parties of thieves from surrounding clans. But although it had kept their cattle safe, it had proved a death trap for the thirty-four Struans who'd been slaughtered by the Government troops after the Battle of Culloden.

There was a simple cairn at the far end of the glen to commemorate the infamous day when the MacAllisters, supporters of the Hanoverian King George, had betrayed the hiding-place of the defeated rebel Struans to the troops of Butcher Cumberland.

It might have all happened two hundred and fifty years ago, but in a country where short tempers and long memories were the rule it might have happened yesterday. At least that was what her father had brought her up to believe. MacAllisters, like leopards, never changed their spots.

They got back into the Land Rover and began the precipitous descent to the floor of the glen. The road down at least had been engineered more carefully, with proper drainage to prevent it being undermined and washed away during the winter months.

The sun was now beating down from a cloudless sky, and as they made their way towards the first of the chalets she thought that the glen had never looked prettier. This was one part of the estate MacAllister would love to get his hands on, she thought. When the recession was over and the rich foreign tourists were no longer afraid to fly this place would be a gold mine.

They checked the chalets one by one, making a note of anything that needed doing. The severe winter hadn't done as much damage as she'd feared.

Lachie finally tested the big diesel generator that supplied electric power. The wealthy businessmen who came here liked to pretend they were roughing it by hunting and shooting in the wilds, but they still demanded their microwave ovens, electric blankets and satellite TV.

Finally they took a break and sat in the Land Rover enjoying the coffee and sandwiches Morag had prepared that morning. On the dashboard the speaker of the CB radio crackled and a garbled voice came and faded. They ignored it. There was too much interference over these things nowadays as the Cellnet network extended its coverage of the country. When the time was right she'd have to see about acquiring mobile hand-held phones for use around the estate.

Lachie glanced at the list of repairs and grunted, 'A couple of days' work at the most should put things to right. We've been lucky. I thought all those storms during the winter would have caused more damage. Your father really built these chalets to last.'

The hot coffee was scalding her lips and she blew into the cup. 'Aye. Rory never did anything by halves. All we need now are the customers.' She glanced sideways at him. 'I suppose Morag told you about our little discussion the other night?'

'She did. She mentioned that you were having a bit of trouble with Dirk.' He chewed on a sandwich thoughtfully, then gulped it over and said, 'Mind you, she doesn't talk much, but when she does she's usually worth listening to.'

She braced herself for the worst. 'Morag thinks I should marry Dirk. Is that a roundabout way of telling me that you agree with her?'

'I never said that.'

'So you disagree with her?'

'I never said that either.'

She refused to get exasperated with him. If he didn't want to commit himself that was his privilege, and she had too much respect for him to make a big issue out of it. Anyway, he was no expert on matrimony. His own wife had left him many years ago to return to the softer life down south.

He took a drink of his coffee then glanced at her again. 'Why don't you ask me what I think of Dirk MacAllister?'

She smiled to herself. You really had to admire the man's diplomacy. 'All right, then, Lachie. What do you think of Dirk MacAllister? From a man's point of view, of course.'

Lachie considered his answer carefully then said, 'From a man's point of view Dirk MacAllister is someone you don't want to get on the wrong side of. He can be a dangerous enemy.'

She nodded in triumph. 'Just what I thought. He's nothing but a ruthless——'

He cut her off abruptly. 'Don't you go putting words into my mouth. I said no such thing.'

'You said he was dangerous,' she protested.

'Aye. And so can you be when you get riled up. I've seen you waving shotguns around. You're a damned menace at times.' He paused. 'But you're not ruthless and neither is he. You both know when to draw the line.' He paused then added acidly, 'The only

man I've ever known around here who could be called
ruthless was your own late father.'

The remark had an oddly disturbing effect, and she
frowned at him. 'Morag called him a sly old devil and
now you say he was ruthless. Is there something about
Rory's past that you're both keeping from me?'

He turned to look at her, his face giving nothing
away. 'He was your father. You should know what
he was like better than anyone. Anyway, I thought
we were discussing Dirk?'

It was evident from the grim set of his mouth that
he wasn't going to be drawn, so she gave up trying.

'I know how dangerous an enemy he can be,' she
said, getting back to the subject. 'Either I marry him
or he's going to make me bankrupt.'

'Well, at least he's giving you a choice,' Lachie said
shrewdly. 'If he was as ruthless as you think he is he'd
just bankrupt you and that would be the end of it.'

This wasn't getting her anywhere, she thought de-
spondently, but perhaps that was her own fault. Was
she really interested in anyone else's opinion of Dirk,
or was she looking to others simply to confirm her
own low estimation of the man? She had enough justification as it was for hating him. Did she really need
to go looking for more?

'Dirk's father. Old Blackie. Now there was a real
bloody-minded old villain,' Lachie reminisced.
'Everyone hated him. The mothers in Kinvaig used
to frighten their bairns by telling them that old Blackie
would come and take them away if they didn't behave
themselves. A brute of a man. As big as your father.
The old-timers will tell you of the day Rory accused
him of cheating him over a cattle sale and they fought
for two solid hours on the pier. Neither would give

in, and in the end it took six men to pull them apart before they killed one another.

'Later on, when Dirk was about eighteen years old, old Blackie started going downhill. He grew too fond of the whisky and let the estate fall into debt. Dirk took over. Blackie still thought that he was in charge, but it was Dirk who managed to get the place back on its feet again. Now that Blackie is gone the estate is the best run and most profitable in the county. Dirk really knows the business.'

'He's a good businessman right enough,' she admitted sullenly. 'It's his business methods I'm not too keen on—extortion and blackmail. He's a one-man Mafia.'

Lachie finished his coffee and screwed the top back on the flask with an air of finality. 'You were the one who asked me what I thought of Dirk MacAllister, and I'm telling you. I can't help it if you don't like the answers. All I know is that he's always been decent to his estate workers. At least he's honest and generous and you won't find——'

'Generous!' She raised an eyebrow in disbelief. 'Dirk MacAllister, generous? You're talking about the man who's trying to ruin me, for God's sake!'

Lachie shook his head. 'I can't see it. It's not like him. Anyway, don't take my word for it. Go down to Kinvaig and ask the Reverend Mr MacLeod who it was who put up the money for the new youth club . . . or who supplies the food and drink for the old folks' monthly ceilidh.'

She bit her lip and stared miserably across the Glen. Lachie was right; she definitely didn't like the answers she was getting. She was going to end up actually admiring Dirk MacAllister if she listened to much more of this. She'd be forgetting what he'd done to her or how he'd been indirectly responsible for the death of her father.

Suddenly she challenged him in a voice of barely contained resentment, 'If he's as good and generous as you're making him out to be, how is it that Rory had no time for him? My father was a pretty good judge of character.'

'Not when it came to Dirk,' Lachie said emphatically. 'Dirk is a MacAllister and that was enough for Rory.'

At the beginning of the following week she received an overdue cheque through the post, and her spirits rose. Perhaps it was a sign of better things to come. It was good to feel solvent, even if just for a little while, and she decided that for a change she'd go into Kinvaig in style. Scorning her usual garb of Aran sweater and jeans, she donned a beige, two-piece linen suit with white silk blouse.

Morag eyed the transformation in approval. 'It's nice to see that you can still look like a lady now and again if you put your mind to it.'

Unperturbed by the two-edged compliment, she merely smiled sweetly and swept past her.

Kinvaig was busy that morning. Down by the pier a couple of boats were loading up with ice and empty fish boxes beneath a cloud of wheeling gulls. She parked the jeep by the sea wall then crossed the road to the bank. She deposited the cheque, then on the strength of it drew some money from her deposit account and made straight for the garage to settle her outstanding bill with Stewart.

She was glad to get that burden off her mind, and her step was even lighter as she made for her next port of call. It had been a long time since she'd spent anything on herself, and this morning she was determined to be utterly self-indulgent for once. It might be a long time before she'd ever be able to treat herself again.

The Kinvaig Emporium had originally been a chandler store catering mostly for the needs of the fishing fleet, but as the number of boats had diminished and the demands of the tourists increased the store had quadrupled in size and now sold everything from fishing tackle to designer knitwear and exquisite pieces of Caithness glassware. Shona had always found it more convenient to buy her clothes there than make the trip to Inverness. In any case, the quality was far better than anything you'd find in a city store.

Kirsty McEwan, the middle-aged matron in charge of the clothing department, greeted her with her usual deference. 'How nice to see you, Miss Struan. Isn't the weather lovely? And how is yourself and Morag keeping these days?'

Shona smiled. This was the way of life up here. Whether you were buying a new car or a daily newspaper, good manners dictated that the proper rituals must be observed first.

'Morag and I are fine, Kirsty. And yourself?'

'A wee touch of arthritis last January, but at my age that's only to be expected.'

'Well, I'm sorry to hear that, Kirsty. Try eating lots of mackerel. When I was at university I met an old doctor who used to swear by it.'

'Is that so? Well, I might give it a try. Now, was there something you were needing or are you just in for a browse?'

'I'm not sure I really need anything, Kirsty. I just felt like giving myself a wee treat, if you know what I mean.'

Kirsty nodded wisely. 'Och, aye. And I'm sure you deserve it.'

'I'm sure she does, also,' drawled a voice from the doorway. Shona stiffened and rigidly turned to see Dirk grinning at her.

Kirsty gave him a friendly wave. 'I'll be with you in a moment, Mr MacAllister.'

'There's no hurry, Kirsty. It's Shona I came to see. I saw her jeep and guessed she'd be in here.'

Shona tightened her lips, determined to act as if he weren't there in spite of the fact that he'd strolled over and was now standing by her elbow. Trust him to spoil her morning, she thought bitterly. Just when she imagined that things were looking a little rosier he had to turn up and remind her of her troubles.

Kirsty was enthusing about some new Shetland wool jumpers she had in stock. Shona, who had suddenly lost all interest, quickly chose two, and as soon as they were wrapped and paid for she pushed past Dirk and marched out of the shop.

He caught up with her just as she was tossing the parcels into the rear seat of the jeep. 'Didn't you hear me back there?' he demanded. 'I said I wanted to talk to you.'

She glared up into his gunmetal-grey eyes and hissed, 'Take your hand off my arm. I don't want people to get the impression that we're friends.'

Her hostility caused a momentary flash of anger in his eyes, then he gave a relaxed grin. 'You and I have unfinished business. You left the house in such a hell of a temper the other night. I'd hoped you'd have cooled down and thought it over by now.'

'I have,' she grated. 'And the answer is still, "Drop dead". And if you don't let go of my arm I'm going to kick you on the shins.'

Her threat, which she was quite ready to carry out, merely put another amused twist to his lips.

'Still the little fire-cracker, I see. I'm really going to enjoy taming you when the time comes.' He released her arm, but placed his hand on the jeep door, barring her way. 'Tell me, Shona, do you ever act like a reasonably intelligent woman or are you a permanent victim to that vicious temper of yours?'

She contented herself by continuing to glare at him in stony silence. The last thing she wanted was to get involved in any kind of conversation with him. Silent contempt was the treatment from now on.

'I've got a proposition for you. I think we should discuss it.' He nodded in the direction of the hotel. 'We can discuss it in there over an early lunch.'

She pressed her lips firmly shut and closed her eyes. Only the fear of appearing childish prevented her from jamming her hands over her ears. Go away, her mind screamed at him. Leave me alone.

He heaved a sigh. 'That's a pity.' He paused then added casually, 'What would you like me to do with the bra you left in my library? Shall I give it to Mrs Ross? She can always pass it on to Morag the next time they meet.'

Her eyes jerked open in horror. 'Bra?'

'Yes. The one you left on the library floor.' His grey eyes mocked her unmercifully. 'Don't you remember? It got torn and you were in such a hurry to get dressed that you didn't bother to put it on.'

Oh, yes, she remembered all right! Not at the time, but when she'd arrived home and gone for a shower...

'You're lucky I was the one to find it after you'd gone,' he drawled. 'I hate to imagine what Mrs Ross would have made of it. You know how these house-keepers gossip. You'd be known from now on as the scarlet woman of Kinvaig.'

A horrible suspicion bloomed darkly in her mind. 'Where is it now?' she demanded hoarsely. 'I...I don't want it back. Get rid of it. Put it on the fire or something. It's no use to me now.'

'OK. I will if I can only remember where I put it. I may have put it under a cushion, but I'm not sure.' He grinned and her stomach turned over. That calculated look of innocence on his face told her all she wanted to know.

In a frantic hiss she threatened him, 'If Mrs Ross should happen to find it I'll explain it by telling everyone that you tried to rape me. It'll be your word against mine. Then we'll see whose reputation suffers.'

His scornful laugh swept over her like an icy wave. 'I think that my side of the story will sound a lot more credible than yours. Let's consider the facts, Miss Struan. You're in financial trouble and everyone knows it. You turned up at my house desperately begging for a loan. Regretfully I had to refuse. But you wouldn't take no for an answer and you offered me a service which involved the removal of your clothes and the temporary use of your body.'

Her eyes widened in incredulity. 'No one would believe a word...'

'Wouldn't they? Are you sure about that? You certainly weren't raped, otherwise Mrs Ross would have heard your screams and cries for help. And you'd have undoubtedly reported it to someone as soon as you'd made your escape.' He eyed her mockingly. 'Did you?'

She clenched her fists in frustration and fought down the rising bile in her throat. 'There are no depths you won't sink to to get your own way, are there?'

He put his face close to hers and whispered provocatively, 'Not when the prize is as lusciously desirable as you.'

She turned her head away from those deeply disturbing eyes and tried to loosen the strange tightness in her chest with a deep breath. 'Just exactly what is it you want from me now?'

'I told you. A quiet lunch in the hotel. That's not too much to ask from a friend and neighbour, is it?'

Unless she was prepared to call his bluff about the bra her best course of action was to get this over and done with as soon as possible. Allowing her shoulders to slump dejectedly, thus making it plain to him that she was only obliging him under protest, she muttered, 'All right. But I'm warning you now, I'm not listening to any of your propositions. You'll just be wasting your time.'

'We'll see.' He took her firmly by the elbow and led her along the seafront to the hotel restaurant entrance.

The dining-room was empty and after waiting for a few moments he rang the bell impatiently. A full minute passed before the manager wandered in, and at the sight of Dirk his face fell. Dirk looked at him coldly and snapped, 'From now on I want someone on permanent duty in here whether there are any customers or not. Now get someone to take our order and then see about getting some heating in this place.'

As he chose a table and assisted her into her seat she put a disdainful curl to her lip. 'You like to throw your weight around, don't you? Just because you own the place you don't have to act like Attila the Hun.'

'I'll act any way I see fit to look after my investment,' he growled.

Their eyes clashed over the table until hers wavered and fell away.

'This is supposed to be a restaurant,' he reminded her tolerantly. 'At the moment the room is cold and I had to call for service. When customers come in here I want them to receive a warm, friendly welcome and the best of attention, so that they'll remember the place and come back. If I have to throw my weight around to achieve that standard that's exactly what I'll do.'

A waiter scurried in with a menu, but Dirk didn't even glance at it. Instead he smiled at her. 'I recommend the venison in red wine sauce.'

Quiet rebellion simmered in her voice. 'I'm not hungry.'

'All right. We'll have some wine first.' He glanced up at the waiter. 'A bottle of claret, please. We'll order later.'

When the waiter had gone she scowled at him over the table. 'I remember what happened the last time I came in here with you. Do you blame me for not having any appetite?'

He sat back in his chair, completely relaxed and sure of himself. 'Don't lie to yourself, Shona. It was

the most wonderful day of your life. And mine. With
any luck we might get to repeat it.'

The man's conceit was unbearable. 'I might also
grow another head,' she remarked coldly. 'You never
know what they're putting in the food these days.'

'I might grow on you if you give me half a chance,'
he drawled lazily. 'All this needless hostility is getting
boring, and life's too short for that.'

'You're the one who caused the hostility in the first
place,' she reminded him tartly.

'And I'm the one who's now trying his damnedest
to end it,' he retorted.

'By trying to blackmail me into marriage?' Her
smile was as contemptuous as she could make it.
'You'll pardon me if I find that funny, won't you?'

The accusation brought a puzzled frown to his face.
'What the hell are you talking about?'

He was going to deny it now, she thought bitterly,
either deny it or try to twist his words around. Her
father had been right about the MacAllisters. They
were as cunning and unscrupulous as foxes.

'You know perfectly well what I'm talking about,'
she charged. 'If I don't marry you you'll make me
bankrupt and take my estate from me.'

His grey eyes widened fractionally in surprise, then
he gave a sigh of exasperation and appealed to the
ceiling. 'God help me. The woman I want as a wife
is a fool.'

'Don't you call me a fool,' she said furiously. 'I
can believe my own ears, can't I?'

'Well, I can't believe mine. What makes you think
I want that useless piece of peat bog and——?'

She got to her feet and glared at him. 'First you
call me a fool, then you call my land a useless peat

AND HIT THE JACKPOT!

Up to 4 free Romances, a Teddy and a Mystery Gift. ▶

HOW TO PLAY 421

GREAT FREE GAME WITHOUT OBLIGATION TO BUY

1 With a coin, scratch the 3 silver dice opposite and discover in an instant whether you will receive... 2, 3 or maybe 4 free books and perhaps 1 or 2 extra gifts.

To claim the Jackpot, it is sufficient that your dice display 4, 2, 1 in any order.

2 When you return the card to us, you will receive as many free Romances as you have revealed and perhaps also a cuddly Teddy and a Mystery Gift.

3 If we don't hear from you within 10 days, we'll send you 6 brand new Romances for just £1.80 each every month. You will of course be under no obligation and may cancel or suspend your subscription at any time by simply dropping us a line.

Mills & Boon Reader Service, Freepost, PO Box 236, Croydon, Surrey. CR9 9EL.
Registered Office: 18-24 Paradise Road, Richmond, Surrey. TW9 1SR
Registered in England No. 100449

Here is the cuddly Teddy that you could receive if you hit the Jackpot!

If you claim your free books we'll also send you this appealing little Teddy absolutely FREE. Soft and cuddly, he's a favourite with everyone.

PLAY 421 WITH MILLS & BOON

Scratch the 3 silver dice and see instantly which gifts you will receive.

YES! Please send me all the free books and gifts to which I am entitled and reserve me a Reader Service subscription. I understand that I am under no obligation to purchase anything ever. If I do not wish to receive 6 brand new Mills & Boon Romances every month for just £1.80 each, I simply write and let you know within 10 days. If I choose to subscribe to the Mills & Boon Reader Service I will receive 6 brand new Romances for just £10.80 every month. There is no charge for postage and packing. I may cancel or suspend my subscription at anytime simply by writing to you. The free books and gifts are mine to keep in anycase. *I am over 18 years of age.*

MS/MRS/MISS/MR ————————————————————

ADDRESS ————————————————————

————————————————————

POSTCODE ——————————— SIGNATURE ———————————

12A3R

**4 FREE BOOKS
+ A CUDDLY TEDDY
AND A MYSTERY GIFT.**

**4 FREE BOOKS
+ A CUDDLY TEDDY.**

3 FREE BOOKS.

2 FREE BOOKS.

<u>To claim</u>
<u>421 can be in any order</u>

MAILING PREFERENCE SERVICE

THE MILLS & BOON GUARANTEE

- You will not have any obligation to buy.
- You have the right to cancel at any time.
- Your gifts remain for you to keep in any case.

bog! I didn't come in here to listen to your insults, and if you think for one minute——'

'For God's sake sit down and behave yourself,' he said wearily. 'I apologise. You aren't a fool and your estate is wonderful. Most of it is wasteland, but Glen Gallan makes up for that. I hope you do manage to keep it, because I certainly don't want the responsibility for keeping it solvent.'

She looked at him uncertainly. This had to be another one of his tricks.

He pointed to her chair. 'Sit.'

She sat.

He nodded. 'That's better. Now let's get the facts straight, shall we?' She felt as if she was back in school again, getting a tongue-lashing for not doing her homework. Colour burned in her cheeks as he went on, 'Unless something happens pretty soon you're going to have to sell up.'

She swallowed painfully. 'Perhaps . . .'

'There's no perhaps about it,' he said in a voice that suggested that he was sick and tired of the whole business. 'If you don't stop deluding yourself you're just going to get deeper into trouble.'

He paused as the waiter returned with the wine. Dirk poured two glasses, handed one to her, and after a moment's hesitation she took a sip. Now she was drinking with the enemy, she thought guiltily. Thank heaven Rory wasn't here to see this.

As soon as the waiter was out of earshot Dirk relaunched his attack. 'All I want from you is an agreement that if you do have to sell you'll sell to me and no one else.'

Her eyes narrowed with suspicion. 'If it's just a useless peat bog as you said, why are you so anxious to get your hands on it? It doesn't make sense.'

'Because I don't want strangers up here.' They eyed each other in silence. It sounded like a pretty feeble excuse to her, and her look of scepticism clearly didn't amuse him.

'Look,' he snapped, 'I don't want to see some big development corporation coming up here and turning the area into a second-rate copy of Disneyland. If you sell to me things will stay exactly as they are, with you in charge.'

Her mind raced, searching and probing for the hidden pitfall. There had to be one somewhere. Finally she shook her head. 'I don't believe you.'

'Why?' he asked drily. 'Because you believe the MacAllisters have always been congenital liars?'

She nodded. 'Something like that. Bitter experience has taught me how much your promises are worth.'

His lean features grew hard, and his grey eyes became bleak and wintry. 'I've been thinking about that, Miss Struan. I asked you to marry me because I thought that I was in love with you and that we'd get along together, but now I'm beginning to wonder. What I did five years ago may have been for the best after all. It seems to me now that you're just an ignorant, vindictive little fool who deserves all that's coming to her.'

His hand shot across the table and grabbed her wrist, anticipating her intention of throwing her drink in his face.

'What kind of life would I have married to you, eh?' he demanded harshly. 'You think of no one but yourself. The only thing in the world you care about is your obnoxious pride in being a Struan.'

His savage tirade shook her to the core and she stammered, 'Th . . . that isn't true.'

'Isn't it?' His eyes lanced into the dark depths of her soul. 'Only a few minutes ago you were threatening to have me charged with a rape that you know never happened. You'd rather see me rot in prison for seven years than run the risk of having people gossip about you. Is that the Struan idea of fair play and justice?'

She lowered her eyes in shame and muttered, 'I . . . I didn't mean it. It was just a threat made in anger.'

He released her wrist and said sourly, 'Aye. There's too much of your father in you. You never stop to think. You get in a temper, a red mist covers your eyes, and you lash out regardless of the consequences.'

She pushed her glass away and got shakily to her feet. 'I . . . I think I'd better go.'

'Sit down,' he barked. 'I'm not finished with you yet.'

Completely dominated by the sheer force of his personality, she sank unprotesting back into her seat.

He sat regarding her in a thoughtful silence which dragged on and became positively unnerving. She'd never be a match for this man, but her spirit wasn't completely crushed yet.

'You don't deserve it,' he growled at last, 'but I'm going to give you one last chance. If you turn it down, then you're a bigger fool than I thought.'

The fingers of his right hand beat a tattoo on the tablecloth as he awaited her answer, but she continued to stare at him in a numb, white-faced silence. The way he'd gone about assassinating her character had been nothing short of brutal, and she still couldn't trust her voice.

He smiled coldly at her obvious discomfort, then he put his proposition in a brisk, businesslike manner. 'I'm prepared to give you an interest-free loan for a period of eighteen months. Enough to see you through the next two seasons. It'll be a strictly private loan and you won't have to put up anything in the way of security. If you can't repay the loan after eighteen months I'm prepared to write it off, but you'll have to sell the estate to me. The conditions will remain the same. Nothing changes. You'll still be in charge. I may make a few improvements around the place, but that's all. Our lawyers can draw up an agreement and you can have it in writing.'

Once more her mind raced. On the face of it it was a ridiculously generous offer, almost too generous to be true. But could she accept it? There was one fact that was too unpalatable to swallow. Even if everything still remained the same and she was left in charge it would be his name on the title deeds of the land that had belonged to her ancestors for generations. Was she prepared to live with the knowledge that she'd been the one to end it all?

Her eyes grew hot with resentment as she stared at him across the table. He was the man who had caused her and her father such pain and heartache. Was she now going to have to surrender and let him win without a fight? Did she have any choice?

'I can't give you my answer now,' she said with quiet bitterness. 'I'll have to think it over.'

He shrugged. 'Do that. Talk to your lawyer. But don't take too long...' His voice trailed off as the door burst open and a tousle-haired twelve-year-old stumbled in.

The boy looked at Shona and gasped, 'Miss Struan...'

Dirk got to his feet and said quietly, 'Calm down, Kevin. What's the problem?'

The boy was shaking with excitement. 'The CB...in the jeep. Lachie...says to tell you the poachers are back.'

Her eyes widened in a sudden blazing anger and her chair was overturned as she leapt to her feet and made a dash for the door.

CHAPTER SIX

WITH her long legs flying and her skirt halfway up her thighs, Shona raced towards the jeep, but Dirk still managed to beat her to it. As he settled himself in the driving seat she glared at him, breathless and indignant. 'That's my jeep. Get out right now or I'll——'

Ignoring her protest, he switched on the handmike. 'Lachie? Dirk here. Where are they?'

Lachie's voice crackled from the speaker. 'Donnie's Pool. They're using gelignite. It's the same transit van that was here last time.'

'I'm with Shona. We'll be there as quick as we can.' He switched off then looked up at her impatiently. 'Don't just stand there like an idiot. Get in.'

'This is none of your business, MacAllister,' she fumed. 'They're poaching on my property, not yours.'

He shook his head in disbelief. 'Don't be so bloody stupid. Donnie's Pool might be on your property, but the whole of the river isn't. Some of the fishing stretches belong to me, and the bloody salmon don't know the difference, do they?'

'All right,' she conceded angrily. 'But you can use your own car.'

'It's in the garage having new brake shoes fitted,' he snapped. 'Now get in or I'll leave you standing there.' To emphasise his threat he started the engine and gunned the accelerator noisily.

Her feelings of animosity towards him were far outweighed by the hatred she felt for the poachers. Lachie had said that they were using gelignite, so that meant they were killing fish on an enormous scale. One stick of explosive tossed into a pool stunned the fish and they simply floated to the surface to be collected at leisure. Using that method, they could clear a whole stretch of river in an hour. These people were wrecking her already precarious means of livelihood. If there were no fish in the river for the tourists and anglers to catch they'd stop coming and she would lose future income.

Dirk engaged first gear and she scowled at him. 'All right. Wait till I get in, damn you.'

She'd barely had time to secure her seatbelt when he let out the clutch and the jeep leapt forward. Halfway round the bay there was a hump-backed bridge where the road crossed the mouth of the river, and for a few seconds the jeep was airborne before it thudded back on to the road with a spine-jarring jolt. He wrenched at the steering-wheel and skidded right at the T-junction, spraying grass and gravel from the verge.

Her knuckles whitened and she yelled at him, 'You damned maniac! Let's try and get there in one piece, shall we?'

'You can get out and walk if you like,' he shouted back.

She clamped her mouth shut, folded her arms across her chest, and stared furiously ahead. The road up this glen was narrow, twisting and treacherous if taken at speed. A blown tyre or a mistimed gear change could send them hurtling down the steep embankment into the frothing river below. Her life was now literally in his hands, so this wasn't the time to distract his attention with arguments.

Ignoring her present danger, she focused her mind on the problem of how to deal with the poachers when they caught up with them. Lachie and she had caught three of them last year. Lachie had had to keep threatening them with his shotgun until she'd managed to contact the police in Inverness. Then it had taken the police two hours to arrive.

But supposing the poachers were armed themselves this time? In the old days they usually surrendered without an argument, but lately they'd been resorting more and more to violence.

She had no doubt of Lachie's courage and determination, but what about MacAllister? He was good when it came to throwing his weight around with women or people who couldn't fight back, but he certainly had proved that he hadn't had the guts to stand up to her father. Would he be in such a hurry now if he didn't know that Lachie was already there to back him up? She doubted it.

They'd gone about another two miles when they saw Lachie standing by his Land Rover, and Dirk drew the jeep alongside.

There was a look of grim satisfaction on Lachie's face as he explained the situation. 'We've got the bastards now. There are five of them and they've parked their van in the old quarry just past the pool. They're there now, wondering who the hell let the air out of their tyres.'

Shona reached across to the CB radio and lifted the mike, but Dirk stopped her with a frown and snapped, 'What are you doing?'

'I'm going to call Morag at the house,' she said impatiently. 'She can phone from there to the police at Inverness.'

He dismissed that idea with a contemptuous snort. 'We don't need the police. We can deal with this ourselves.'

She looked him up and down with derision. 'Don't be ridiculous. You heard Lachie. There are five of them.'

Dirk nodded grimly. 'I heard. But it makes no difference. These scum aren't going to be stopped just because a court fines them. It'll just make them more careful the next time they pay us a visit.'

'I'm aware of that,' she informed him coldly. 'But we don't have any choice in the matter, do we? All we can do is make a citizen's arrest and wait for the police to arrive. That's the law. It might not be justice, but it's the law nevertheless.'

The ironic smile on his lips taunted her. 'I'm surprised at you, Shona. Rory would never have waited on the police. He had his own way of dealing with situations like this and so have I.'

'Aye...' Lachie interrupted drily. 'And while the pair of you are discussing it the poachers are pumping up their tyres ready for a getaway.'

'Have you got another gun in the Land Rover?' Dirk asked him.

'Aye. Young Jamie's.'

As he went to fetch it she looked at Dirk with exasperation, resenting the way he was imposing himself and taking charge of the proceedings. They were her fish and her poachers and he had no damned right interfering, but one look at that bleak countenance told her that she'd be as well arguing with a slab of granite.

As he took the extra gun from Lachie and placed it on the back seat she remarked sourly, 'You'll feel a lot tougher with that in your hands, I suppose?'

'The gun is for you,' he growled. 'For your own personal protection. You were quick enough to threaten me with one, so don't pretend you're squeamish.'

The quarry, hidden from the road by a curved entrance, was the ideal place for concealment, and the poachers stood frozen in surprise as the jeep and Land Rover suddenly roared in and skidded to a halt beside one another.

They were about five of the meanest-looking brutes Shona had ever seen in her life. Casually she got out of the jeep and cradled the shotgun in her arms, then watched with interest as Dirk walked menacingly over to the transit van. Her own plan of action would have been to block the quarry entrance with the two vehicles and wait for the police to arrive, but MacAllister obviously had other ideas.

By now Lachie was out of the Land Rover with his shotgun and she went over to join him. 'Do you recognise any of them, Lachie?'

'Aye. That big, dark one with the scar on his face. They're the same gang as was here last time.'

Dirk yanked open the back door of the van, glanced inside, then barked an order. 'Right, you lot! Start unloading these salmon and put them in the Land Rover.'

The poachers exchanged glances, then the one with the scar on his cheek sneered, 'There are five of us and only two of you.'

'Three,' Dirk corrected. 'Don't ignore the lady. It upsets her.'

The leader grinned at his mates then leered at Shona. 'We know how to deal with women, don't we, lads? Especially sexy-looking redheads.'

'Watch your mouth,' Dirk warned softly.

The man ignored him. 'We can always do a deal. We'll give you the fish back if you lend her to us for half an hour. She looks like she'd enjoy a good——'

Dirk made a lunge for him, but Shona yelled, 'Dirk! Wait!' White-faced with rage, she strode forwards, the shotgun pointing straight at the leader. Viciously she pushed the barrel into his stomach and abused him in a torrent of Gaelic.

The man stumbled backwards, fear widening his eyes, but she kept up the pressure. Suddenly she swung the gun round, pointed it at the rear wheel of the van, and pulled the trigger. The tyre disintegrated in the explosion, and pieces of smouldering rubber went sailing through the air.

The echoes of the shot died away and there was a shocked silence, then Dirk grinned at the gang leader. 'We don't use filthy words like that here. You've obviously upset the lady. Now unless you want to lose bits of your anatomy you'd better do as you're told from now on.'

Scowling and muttering to themselves, the gang stumbled and tripped over each other in their haste to transfer the fish to the Land Rover.

When they'd finished Dirk made them line up against the transit, then he eyed them savagely. 'I'm not going to involve the police in this. What I was going to do was wreck your van, take your shoes, and make you walk barefoot to the nearest main road.

That's only twenty-five miles from here. But I've changed my mind.' He pointed his finger at the leader. 'You insulted a lady. You all did, and you're going to pay for it. By the time I've finished with you you'll never come north of Fort William again. I'm going to thrash the lot of you. One by one.'

Shona frowned. What the devil was he talking about? Anyway, she didn't need him to fight her battles. She could give as good as she got. There were bits of rubber tyre all over the place to prove it.

The poachers grinned at one another and the leader sneered, 'And what happens if you can't manage to take all five of us on? Are the police still out of it?'

Dirk already had his jacket off and he smiled coldly. 'That's the idea. You're the biggest and ugliest. Would you like to be first?'

Lachie levelled his gun at them and said quietly, 'One at a time, gentlemen, if you don't mind.'

The lout needed no second invitation and he hurled himself like a juggernaut at Dirk. Shona stood open-mouthed at the scene, then gulped as Dirk stepped aside and stuck his foot out. The man sprawled his length on the ground, then got up, spitting and snarling, before trying another mad rush. This time Dirk caught him squarely between the eyes with his left fist then swung his right at the exposed jaw. There was a tremendous crack and the man's eyes glazed before he sank to the ground and stayed there.

Dirk ignored him, then pointed his finger at another of the gang. 'You're next.'

'You've got to hand it to him,' chuckled Lachie. 'He's a bonny fighter. Just like his father, old Blackie.'

It was too much for Shona. She fired the second barrel in the air then shouted, 'That's enough! You come here this instant, Dirk MacAllister. I want to talk to you.'

He came over to her, his displeasure at her intervention plain to see.

'Are you mad?' she spat at him. 'They're nothing but gutter trash and you're descending to their level. If you must act like a hooligan do it on your own property, not mine.'

The remorseless savagery in his eyes turned to mere annoyance at being thwarted. 'It's the only thing they understand, dammit!'

'He's right,' observed Lachie judicially. 'Don't you go spoiling the fun, now.'

She glared from one to the other. 'You're worse than schoolboys, the pair of you.'

Dirk nursed his right fist and growled, 'You're a woman. You don't understand these people. Violence is the only thing they respect.'

'You're right,' she said with heavy sarcasm. 'I am a woman, thank God. And I know how to deal with people like them without forgetting the fact. I can make sure they never dare show their faces here again, and I can do it without laying a finger on them.'

Dirk and Lachie frowned at her. 'How?'

'Just leave that to me.'

Lachie eyed Dirk and shrugged. 'You'd better let her have her way. If you don't she'll just make my life miserable, because I'll never hear the end of it.'

Dirk looked her over reluctantly then sighed. 'OK. Do it your way.'

'Well, thanks very much,' she grated. 'I must say it's nice of you to let me do what I want on my own land.' She nodded towards the van. 'Lachie, put a shot in the radiator.'

The gang edged away nervously from the van and the leader got groggily to his feet. There was another explosion and water spurted from the shattered radiator.

Looking at the poachers disdainfully, she gave them their orders. 'You're going to start walking to Kinvaig. It's four miles. Follow the Land Rover. I'll be right behind you in the jeep.'

Grumbling among themselves, they dutifully followed Lachie out of the quarry in a straggling line. She sat in the passenger seat of the jeep while Dirk drove at walking pace.

'You're a danger to yourself, MacAllister,' she scoffed after they'd gone about half a mile. 'You'd never have finished the five of them. The first two, maybe, but you'd have been in trouble after that.'

He grinned. 'How do you know? I was doing fine until you stopped me.'

'Look at the knuckles of your right hand. They're red and swollen. I wouldn't be surprised if something isn't broken or dislocated.'

He flexed his right hand on the steering-wheel and she detected the tiny grimace of pain at the corner of his mouth.

'Stop the jeep,' she said. 'I'll drive.'

They changed places, then, before engaging the gear, she paused and searched under the dashboard for a clean rag. Scrambling down the embankment, she dipped the rag in the cold water of the river then returned to the jeep.

'Give me your hand.'

He raised an eyebrow. 'Is that a proposal, at last?'

'Don't be funny,' she snapped. She wrapped the rag around his knuckles. 'That'll keep the swelling down.'

Lachie's voice came over the CB. 'What's wrong back there?'

'Nothing but a little first aid,' she said into the mike. 'We'll catch up in a moment.' She looked up into Dirk's eyes, then impulsively she gave him a quick kiss on the mouth. The temptation to linger was overwhelming, but she resisted it and hurriedly got the jeep moving. 'Don't get any ideas, MacAllister,' she said with the slightest of tremors in her voice. 'That was just to show my appreciation for the way you repaid that man's insulting remark about me.'

Thankfully he didn't pursue the subject, because what she was feeling right now just couldn't be put into words. He'd just proved to her that he was certainly no coward. She doubted if he'd back down from Satan himself. Everything she was hearing and learning about him was wrecking her preconceived notions of the kind of man he was, and it wasn't a comforting thought.

Right now her heart was screaming at her and demanding an answer. If he isn't as bad as you thought, it was saying, then why don't you fall in love with him and stop all this agony?

As she caught up with the procession and slowed the jeep to a walking pace she gave him a quick sideways glance, but not quick enough to escape his notice, and he drawled, 'You didn't have to kiss me, you know. I'd have done the same for any woman.'

She tried to give an indifferent shrug. 'Forget it. I lost my head for a moment. It was just such a surprise to find that there was a bit of a gentleman lurking inside you after all.'

She could feel his eyes mocking her and she swallowed. 'I think you kissed me because you wanted to,' he remarked drily. 'Any excuse would have done. I think that very soon now you're going to have to admit to yourself that you'll never get me out of your system and you'll regret all the time you've wasted.'

'Be quiet,' she snapped. 'Any more talk like that and I'll make you get out and walk beside the rest of those hoodlums.'

He laid his fingers gently on her thigh and stroked it provocatively. 'You wouldn't have the heart to do that, Shona. I've a feeling that the ice maiden is beginning to melt at last.'

Try as she might she couldn't stop her leg trembling nor her heart hammering in her ears. Damn him! He was right. But she wouldn't fall in love with him a second time. She wouldn't allow that to happen for anything.

By the time they reached the harbour in Kinvaig word had spread and the whole village had turned out to witness the proceedings.

The five men were looking at the crowd nervously and offered no argument when she got out of the jeep and ordered them to line up in front of the sea wall. Telling Lachie to keep an eye on them, she pushed her way through the crowd towards the Emporium and had a quick word with Kirsty. Five minutes later she emerged with a large black plastic bag.

Resuming her position in front of the bewildered poachers, she raised her voice so that everyone could hear. 'Lachie, fetch five salmon from the Land Rover.'

The crowd craned their necks and held their breath, wondering what she was up to.

When Lachie brought the fish she told him to lay one at the feet of each of the poachers, and when that was done she smiled at them grimly. 'Well, gentlemen, you seem to have a liking for fish that don't belong to you, so let's see how much you enjoy eating them.'

The one with the scarred face looked at her in disbelief. 'You ain't expecting us to eat raw fish, are you?'

'Not only expecting it but insisting on it,' she said coldly. 'Raw fish is very good for you. The Japanese seem to thrive on it.'

He spat on the ground. 'You're bloody well mad if you think we're going to do that.'

She eyed them in contemptuous silence for a moment, then she nodded. 'Very well. I didn't think you'd do it without a little persuasion.' She signalled to Dirk, who seemed as puzzled as everyone else. 'Tell them to strip. They can keep their shoes and underpants on.'

Dirk's grey eyes lightened with amusement and he confronted the poachers. 'Right! You heard the lady. Take your clothes off.'

Once more the crowd held its breath and the men looked at each other in dismay.

'If you don't do it by yourselves I'll have the village women do it for you,' he warned them grimly. 'They'll be none too gentle about it either, I can assure you. The choice is yours.'

There was a threatening murmur from the crowd, and the men, choosing the lesser of the two evils, began to peel their clothes off. As each article of clothing was dumped at their feet a cheer went up from the crowd.

When that was done she beckoned to two young faces in the crowd and when they rushed up to her she said brightly, 'Ewan . . . Andy . . . I want you to gather up all these clothes and throw them into the sea.'

The two youngsters set about the task with enthusiasm while the poachers looked on in impotent fury. When the job was finished she addressed the men again. 'Your van is out of commission and it's a long, long hike till you come to a main road where you might manage to thumb a lift back to where you came from. It'll get chilly during the night and I don't want any of you to catch pneumonia, so you're each going to get something that'll keep you warm at least.'

She saw the look of relief on their faces then she added coldly, 'I don't want to see you going hungry either. You're going to need all the energy you can get, so I want to see you eating those fish now. If you don't eat, then you don't get the clothes. It's up to you.'

They looked at her in shocked silence, their expressions betraying the stark thoughts that were going through their minds. Eating raw fish might be unpleasant, but the thought of trying to thumb a lift in nothing but their underpants was even worse. One by one they reluctantly picked up the fish and, closing their eyes in disgust, they each took a bite.

To the delight of the crowd Shona walked up and down the line approvingly. 'That's very good. Chew it well before you swallow it. Fish oil is very good for you, they say. That's right. Now another bite . . . no, don't spit it out. You won't get the full benefit that way and it's such a waste of expensive salmon.'

The one at the far end was the first to be sick, and as he dashed for the sea wall the others were quick to follow.

They were a sorry-looking bunch when they turned to face her again. Knowing there was little point in forcing them to eat any more, she rummaged in the bag she'd brought from the Emporium. Once more the crowd was on tiptoe to see what was going to happen next. This was more fun than the annual fishing-queen festival.

Rummaging around in the bag, she drew out a large green dress and threw it at the leader. 'I'm a woman of my word. I promised you something to wear. Try this for size.'

The man held up the dress, then his face darkened. 'I can't wear this!' he exploded.

She looked at him innocently. 'Why? Doesn't green suit you? I admit the style is a bit out of date, but I don't think it's too bad. Anyway, if you don't like it perhaps you can swap with one of your friends.' She pulled the other four dresses from the bag and tossed them at the remaining gang members. As they began to complain her voice hardened and her blue eyes blazed with contempt. 'You've got exactly sixty seconds to put these dresses on or I'll take them back and you'll leave here the way you are.'

The gang knew they were beaten and, avoiding each other's eyes, they struggled into the dresses while the crowd went into fits of hysterical laughter. Amid a racket of catcalls and jeers the five poachers were finally ready, and she spat at them furiously, 'Now you can go and think yourselves lucky. If you ever come up this way again we'll tar and feather you and abandon you on an island for three months.'

With the noise of laughter intensifying their shame, the gang slunk off, their dresses flapping in the wind.

Gradually the crowd dispersed and she asked Lachie to arrange for the remaining salmon to be sent to the fish market at Mallaig, then Dirk caught up with her as she was making for the jeep.

'Where are you going?' he demanded.

The reaction was setting in now and she felt wrung out and exhausted. 'Home. Where do you think? The fun's over now.'

He stared after the disappearing gang of poachers and grinned. 'That was quite a performance. You can't leave now and disappoint the villagers. Apart from that we were about to have a meal before events overtook us.'

She shook her head adamantly. 'I'm still not hungry.'

'Then you'll at least have a drink,' he insisted. 'Half the village is in the hotel bar right now waiting to toast your health. The least you can do is show your face.'

She dug her heels in. 'No. Make some excuse for me. Tell them I'm tired.'

His momentary expression of sympathy quickly became a mask of stern disapproval and he rebuked her harshly, 'Remember who you are. You're Shona Struan and you have a position to maintain around here. It's called *noblesse oblige*. You can't afford to show tiredness. The villagers admire the way you handled those men and they want to show their respect and gratitude.'

She relented with a sigh. 'You can always come up with a good argument, can't you? All right, then. But only one drink, then I'm going home.'

She should have known better.

In a place like this, where a ceilidh lasting two days and nights would be held at the drop of a hat, the rout of the poachers had to be celebrated in style with a party that would be talked about for generations to come.

Escape was impossible. Surrounded at the bar, no sooner had she finished her first drink than someone pushed another glass into her hand and proposed the first of a long line of toasts. Then the furniture was cleared and the music and the dancing began and the ceilidh began in earnest, and there was no way the guest of honour was going to slip off unnoticed.

Even the young ones weren't forgotten. Some of the men set up a barbecue in the hotel car park and the village children were kept happy with a constant supply of sausage, hamburgers and Coke.

Much later she was halfway through another glass of twelve-year-old malt when Dirk pushed his way through the crowd and took it firmly from her hand. 'It's time you had some fresh air. Come outside for a moment.'

Total surprise at his peremptory action robbed her of the power of resistance until they were outside, then she blinked at him in resentment. 'What do you think you're playing at? I was enjoying myself.'

'I could see that. But you don't want to spoil things by getting drunk.'

She felt loose-tongued and light-headed and, drawing herself up indignantly, she said, 'I've never been drunk in my life, I'll have you know.'

'No. And now isn't the time to start.'

'Perhaps I want to,' she retorted defiantly. 'Just once. To see what it's like. And it's none of your damn business anyway. Just leave me alone.'

'You won't find any answers in a bottle,' he said coldly. 'You're wise enough to know that.'

She stared owlishly into his grey eyes, wondering what it was about them that could tear her emotions apart. 'I didn't want to go in in the first place,' she reminded him. 'But you insisted. It was my duty, you said.'

His hand tightened on her arm and he frowned darkly. 'And now I'm insisting that you go home.'

She poked him in the chest with her finger. 'You can insist all you like, Dirk MacAllister, but you don't own any part of me. I'll do what and go where I damn well please.'

Ignoring her taunts, he held out his hand. 'Give me the keys to the jeep.'

She scowled at him. 'No.'

'You'd better let me drive,' he said. 'You're in no fit state.'

'I've no intention of driving,' she said haughtily. 'I'm going to walk home.'

'Good. You won't mind if I accompany you, then?'

She sniffed. 'There's no need. I know the way.'

'Aye,' he said drily. 'I imagine you do since you've lived here all your life. It's still my duty to see you safely home.'

She stuck her nose in the air. 'Please yourself.' It was news to her that he was so zealous about doing his duty. He certainly hadn't been when it had really mattered. Promises and duty were just empty words to him.

She'd only gone a few yards when she sat down on the low sea wall. 'I've got a stone in my shoe,' she mumbled, kicking it off. He bent down, shook out the pebble, gently took her foot in his hand, and replaced the slip-on.

'How's that?'

She stood up and tested her weight. 'Better. Thank you.' She half suppressed a hiccup. 'You can be quite nice when you're not being a cold-hearted pig.' She swayed against his chest and his arms went around her protectively. The warmth of his body and the nearness of his lips weakened her and her eyes refused to meet his. Through the tightness in her throat she sought once more the answer to the question that had haunted and tormented her for so long. 'Why did you do it, Dirk? Why didn't you come for me as you promised? I . . . I used to think that it was because you were afraid of Rory, but I don't believe that any more.'

Gently he stroked her hair. 'I had a very good reason. That's all I can say. I had no option.'

'You had no option but to betray me? Make a fool of me?' She looked up at him now, her eyes filled with sorrow and disbelief.

'It wasn't meant to be like that, Shona.'

She heard the regret and the compassion in his voice, but it wasn't enough to soothe the ache that hurt as much as ever.

'It doesn't matter what you meant it to be,' she said with quiet bitterness. 'That's the way it turned out. I . . . I wish you'd stuck a knife in my heart instead. The pain would have been over in an instant. But it just goes on and on and on.'

He gripped her fiercely by the shoulders and said in a stern voice, 'Then stop being such a stubborn little mule. I'm trying my best to stop the pain, but you won't take the medicine.'

She didn't like the sound of that very much and she pouted her lips. 'Stubborn little mule? Me?'

He dropped his hands helplessly by his side. 'Aye. You.'

She thought it over for a few seconds then expressed her displeasure with a sniff. 'I don't mind being called stubborn—I can handle that—but I've got to draw the line at mule.' She shook her head from side to side. 'No. I definitely do not like being compared to a mule. I think that demands an apology, Mr MacAllister.'

He clicked his heels, bowed his head ever so slightly, then took her hand and kissed it. 'Please accept my profound apologies, Miss Struan. You are not the least bit like a mule.'

She withdrew her hand. 'Thank you, Mr MacAllister. Your apology is accepted.' She hiccuped. 'I beg your pardon. You were right. I was drinking too much.'

'It's hard not to at a ceilidh,' he agreed.

'Yes. It is. I was merely trying to be sociable, you understand. One musn't give the impression that one considers herself too high and mighty to enjoy a drink with one's tenants. Must one?'

He answered her gravely. 'One must certainly not, Miss Struan. Anyway, I wouldn't worry about it. They were all too busy enjoying themselves to pay any attention to how much you were drinking.'

'Except you.' She poked him in the chest with her forefinger again. 'You must have had your beady eye on me all the time.'

He shrugged. 'Let's just say that I felt a certain responsibility since it was I who persuaded you to go in in the first place.'

She cocked her head to the side. 'Is that so? That was very decent of you, Mr MacAllister. Just for that you may kiss me.'

His lips touched hers for a brief, searing moment, then she sighed. 'I wish you weren't so devilishly attractive, Mr MacAllister.'

His eyes regarded her with quiet amusement. 'Oh? Why?'

'Never mind.' She took a deep breath. 'Now, then, what were we talking about? I've forgotten.'

'I called you stubborn,' he reminded her patiently.

'Oh, yes... Well, perhaps it looks that way to you,' she explained loftily. 'I call it pride and self-respect. There's nothing wrong with that, is there? Everyone needs it, don't they?'

'I wouldn't argue with that,' he conceded.

'No. I didn't think you would.' She had him now, the big oaf, she thought with satisfaction. Let him try and wriggle out of this one if he could. With a smile of sly innocence she said, 'I don't think those poachers will ever come back to Kinvaig, do you?'

He gave a dry laugh. 'I shouldn't think so. Not after the showing-up you gave them.'

'Aye. Right. A showing-up. I humiliated them. Took away their self-respect. Made a laughing-stock out of them. That's about the worst thing you can do to anyone. It's worse than a beating.' She began prodding him in the chest again. 'I should know, because that's what you did to me all those years ago. Remember?'

He looked down at her finger and said quietly, 'You're going to break one of my ribs if you keep digging that into me.'

'Huh! Your ribs are more important than my heart?'

They began walking again, and she was only too conscious of his firm grip on her arm. 'You don't have to hold me so tight, you know,' she said crossly. 'I'm not going to fall down or run away.'

He grinned. 'Or hit me?'

She sighed in regret. 'I've already tried that, but it's no use. You're always too quick for me. But don't you worry, Dirk MacAllister. I'm going to get my own back on you one way or another.'

'Then you'll have to wait a couple of weeks at least,' he informed her with a touch of irony. 'I'm leaving for the States tomorrow. I'll be gone for anything up to a month. Perhaps you'll have thought over my proposition by then?'

She had to think what he was talking about for a moment, then she shrugged. 'Perhaps. Perhaps not. Don't hold your breath.'

They were just over halfway to the house when she gave a cry of pain and lurched against him. 'I've twisted my ankle!' She raised her foot and put her hands on his shoulders. 'You'll have to carry me the rest of the way.'

He swept her up and cradled her in his arms. 'No problem. But you'd better hang on.'

She interlaced her fingers behind his neck and rested her cheek against his chest then muttered, 'Don't drop me. I'm feeling fragile.'

'I won't.'

'And don't stop till you get me home,' she warned. 'Not even if you get a pebble in your shoe. Especially if you get a pebble in your shoe.' She smiled up at him. 'I said I'd get my own back, didn't I?'

CHAPTER SEVEN

SHONA had been up on the high moor all day with Lachie and Jamie, and it was late evening when they got home, tired and hungry.

'Your lawyer phoned this afternoon,' Morag told her. 'You've to call him at his home this evening.'

She frowned as she hung her leather jerkin behind the door. 'Did he say what it was about?'

'He's not likely to discuss your private business with your housekeeper, is he?' Morag asked drily. 'Now get yourself cleaned up. Dinner is in half an hour. And don't look so worried, lassie. It's not the end of the world.'

'Oh, aye? And when was the last time MacPhail ever gave me any good news? It'll be more trouble. You can bet on that.'

Under the hot shower the tension left her neck and shoulders, but it did nothing to ease her mind. Why should her lawyer want to contact her by phone? she wondered. Their business together was usually conducted by post—documents to be signed and so forth. Whatever trouble she was in now obviously demanded faster action than the Royal Mail could provide.

She finally donned clean jeans and a checked shirt, but by the time she got back downstairs Lachie and Jamie had already eaten and were nowhere to be seen. Morag served her in silence, then she too found something to occupy her time in another part of the house, leaving Shona to eat her solitary meal feeling as shunned as a plague victim. It was as if they sensed some impending doom and were already wanting to distance themselves from the catastrophe.

She really should have told them about Dirk's offer and her decision to take him up on it. At least it would have settled their minds about the future of the house and the estate. The truth was that she wanted to put it off until the last possible moment in the hope that some miracle would save her from the final climb-down.

Well, they wouldn't have much longer to wait. It was three weeks since Dirk had gone to the States and he'd said he'd be gone a month at most. That meant that within a week at least he'd be back demanding an answer.

In the circumstances she really had no choice but to accept his offer, even if it did mean that she was going to have to live the rest of her life with the knowledge that she'd betrayed her father's memory and had disgraced the name of Struan forever.

She finished her meal and, after piling the dishes in the sink, she went through to the library and phoned her lawyer.

'Ah, Shona! I'm glad you called. How are things going up in Kinvaig?'

He sounded cheerful, which was a change from his usual dry, lugubrious style, and she answered lightly, 'I'm still managing to hang on. But only just.'

'I'm glad to hear it. However, I have good news for you. I think your troubles may be over. There's a man from a London advertising agency arriving tomorrow. He wants to meet you to discuss some sort of deal. Can you be here by three tomorrow afternoon?'

'Yes. Of course.' Her brows came together in a perplexed frown. 'Have you any idea what it's about?'

'I believe it has something to do with Glen Gallan. He wants to use it in some kind of advertising promotion. I'm not quite sure of the details. That's something you'll have to discuss with him yourself.'

She put the phone down thoughtfully. Glen Gallan? Advertising? She shrugged. If it meant extra income for the estate that was all that really mattered. Perhaps this was the miracle she'd been waiting on.

She'd decided to use the Land Rover instead of the jeep for the long trip to Edinburgh, and early next morning Lachie hosed the mud off and checked the engine.

'I don't know if I'll be back tonight,' she told Morag. 'I'm taking a change of clothes in case I decide to stay over. I'll phone you this evening and let you know.'

By ten she was just south of Inverness, the road climbing steeply into the mountains. Near Aviemore she pulled into a lay-by and ate the sandwiches which Morag had prepared, then leisurely sipped at her flask of coffee. A few years ago it would have taken a good six hours from Inverness to Edinburgh, but the recently built dual carriageway cut that time in half, so she had no worries about being late for the appointment.

Last night she'd lain awake wondering why on earth an advertising agency was interested in a remote Scottish glen. Perhaps they wanted to use it as the location for a commercial. Certainly they'd have to ask her permission first, but any fee they might offer for the privilege wouldn't amount to that much. Yet MacPhail had said that her troubles might be over. Finally, no nearer an answer, she gave up and fell asleep.

It was two in the afternoon when she reached Edinburgh, and she parked the Land Rover in the multi-storey at St James's. Her lawyer's office was only a five-minute walk away in York Place, and, not wishing to arrive too early, she spent the time investigating the attractions of the nearby shopping centre.

At the appointed time MacPhail's secretary ushered her into the inner office. Her lawyer arose from behind his desk and extended a hand in welcome. 'Nice to see you again, Shona. I'm glad you could make it on such short notice.'

She smiled politely. 'Your call sounded mysterious. And important. Curiosity got the better of me.' She looked enquiringly at the stranger sitting next to her lawyer. He was a short, energetic-looking type in his middle thirties, wearing a dark suit and aggressively striped shirt.

The man arose and offered her a firm handshake. 'Alan Jacobs of Jacobs and Epstein Advertising, Miss Struan.'

'I'm pleased to meet you Mr Jacobs. Are you going to tell me what this is all about?'

'Certainly.' He glanced at MacPhail. 'Should we wait for Mr MacAllister or get right down to business?'

Her lawyer smiled benevolently. 'Why not give Miss Struan the general outline and——?'

Shona's mouth had dropped open in surprise and now she recovered. 'Just wait a minute! Did I hear something about MacAllister or was it just my imagination?'

Mr Jacobs seemed a little put off by her tone and he glanced quickly at her lawyer before answering. 'Mr MacAllister is my client. It's his product I'm promoting.'

She stared at him in disbelief then looked accusingly at MacPhail. 'What's going on here? You never mentioned MacAllister on the phone. You said that my troubles were over. Now I find that you want me to——'

The door behind her opened and she knew who it was even before she turned. 'You! I thought you were in America.'

His grey eyes surveyed her with calm amusement. 'I arrived back in London three days ago and flew up here this morning. Now, what's all the shouting about?'

She rounded once more on MacPhail. 'Why didn't you tell me that MacAllister was involved in this?'

It was Dirk who answered her in a cold, peremptory voice. 'He was carrying out my orders. If you'd known that I had anything to do with this you wouldn't have come, would you? Now stop shaking your tree and listen to what Mr Jacobs is about to tell you.'

Her mouth opened in violent protest, but he silenced her with a look and said, 'As you can see, Mr Jacobs, Miss Struan isn't the easiest person in the world to get along with. She tends to over-react and be overly suspicious. Just you carry on explaining the deal to her. I'm sure she'll see sense in the end.'

The advertising man was shaken by Shona's unexpected hostility and he cleared his throat nervously.

'The—er—product is intended for an exclusive clientele. Executive boardrooms. Corporate hospitality functions——'

Dirk cut in incisively, 'A picture is worth a thousand words, Mr Jacobs. Isn't that what you advertising people keep telling us? Why don't we show Miss Struan what we're talking about?'

Mr Jacobs blinked then conceded with a smile. 'Yes. Of course.' He reached down into his briefcase, then placed a bottle of whisky on the table. 'This is the product we're discussing, Miss Struan. A very excellent malt whisky distilled by my client Mr MacAllister. Please look at the label.'

With a contrived air of boredom she picked up the bottle. The gold-edged label bore the legend 'Glen Gallan' over a picture of the Glen. 'It's quite pretty,' she agreed finally. She turned her eyes towards Dirk. 'Was this your idea, MacAllister?'

'Aye.' He was frowning at her with impatience. 'Do you like the idea or not, or are you going to take as long as usual to make up your mind?'

'What happens if I don't like it?' she asked caustically.

'Then you'll just be proving yourself to be as foolish and obstinate as ever,' he retorted.

She glared at him, but she hadn't come all this way just to trade insults, so she let it pass, then frowned. 'I presume the whisky is made at your own distillery in Glen Hanish? Why not call it that?'

Dirk gestured to Mr Jacobs and the advertising man explained quickly, 'Glen Gallan sounds more pleasant to the ear, Miss Struan. And the picture of the Glen itself on the bottle. That's going to be a very strong selling point. A real eye-catcher. As Mr MacAllister says, Glen Gallan embodies all the spirit and beauty of the Highlands.'

She inclined her head. 'That may be so. But are you sure this isn't a little bit dishonest? I mean, that bottle of whisky has never been within ten miles of Glen Gallan.' The look she directed at Dirk challenged him to deny her accusation.

Dirk treated her to an ironic smile. 'If you read the label with more attention to detail and less to fault-finding you'll see a statement to the effect that the whisky is actually distilled at Glen Hanish. Since the water in both glens comes from the same source it makes little difference anyway. To put your mind at rest, all the legal implications have already been sorted out. All that remains now is for you to give your permission.'

She looked at her lawyer doubtfully. 'What do you think, Mr MacPhail? You know what Glen Gallan has always meant to the Struans. Should I now let its name be stolen by a MacAllister just so that he can sell more whisky?'

There was an explosive sound of exasperation from Dirk while Mr Jacobs sat with a bemused expression on his face, telling himself, no doubt, that this was the last time he'd ever venture north across the border again to do business with these quarrelsome Scots.

Her lawyer smiled at her uncertainly. 'I don't think Mr MacAllister intends stealing anything, Shona. As I understand it you stand to gain quite substantially from this business proposition.' He glanced at Mr Jacobs for help.

The advertising man caught the ball enthusiastically. At least it was a chance to be seen to be earning his fee. 'You undoubtedly will, Miss Struan. There will be an initial payment once you sign the agreement. But the real benefits will come later. Every bottle of whisky will be sold in an attractive carton. On the side of the carton there will be a brief history of Glen Gallan and a passage dealing with its virtues as the ideal place for a hunting and fishing holiday. The product will be extensively advertised in America, Germany and Japan. In effect your property will get thousands of pounds' worth of publicity and it won't cost you a penny.'

'You'll have to build at least six more chalets to deal with the rush,' Dirk said drily. 'And with the prospects you have before you the banks will be queuing up to lend you money.'

Acutely conscious of three pairs of eyes watching and awaiting her decision, she found it impossible to think straight. If everything she'd heard was above-board, then her troubles really did seem to be over, and yet . . . was that Rory's ghost cursing in her ear? 'I'd like to speak with Mr MacAllister in private,' she told MacPhail at last.

'Of course, my dear. Mr Jacobs and I shall retire next door and have some of Miss Fisher's excellent coffee.'

When they were alone she got to her feet and put her hands on her hips. 'All right, Dirk. What's the catch?'

'Does there have to be a catch?' he asked with thinly concealed bitterness at her attitude.

'Knowing you, I'd bet on it.' She pointed to the bottle on the desk. 'Is that stuff all you claim it to be? I don't want my name connected with some inferior rubbish only fit for stripping paint.'

'You should know. You've already tasted it.' His voice was a lazy drawl of mockery guaranteed to raise her hackles. 'I've been conducting market research at the Kinvaig hotel for the last six months. That's the whisky you were drinking at the ceilidh. As I recall you were enjoying it so much that I practically had to drag you away from the place.'

She flushed at the memory and grumbled, 'You don't have to remind me of that. I don't suppose I'll ever hear the end of it now.'

He surprised her by giving a sympathetic grin. 'There's no need to feel embarrassed about it. You were simply more relaxed and talkative than usual. A bit more uninhibited, shall we say?' He paused then added, 'You were also a wee bit naughty, but we won't dwell on that.'

Indignation flared in her cheeks. 'What do you mean—"naughty"?'

He shrugged. 'Forget it.'

She nearly stamped her foot. 'I won't forget it! You'll have to explain that remark.'

He groaned. 'Don't start poking me with that damn finger again. The bruises from the last time are still there.'

'Then tell me,' she demanded. 'I'm not having you spreading tales about me.'

She kept glaring at him till he gave in. 'All right. The fact is, you were feeling quite amorous towards me, although you tried to——'

'Amorous? Me? Towards you?' She snorted. 'Don't be ridiculous.'

'You pretended that you'd twisted your ankle just so that I'd take you in my arms,' he pointed out.

She spluttered. 'Th...that's not true. I...I really did hurt it.'

Laughter danced across his lips. 'Then why were you limping on the right foot when I picked you up and the left foot when I got you home?'

Her eyes fell away in mortification and she muttered, 'I'm not going to argue with you any more.'

He grinned. 'Glad to hear it. Does that mean you'll sign the agreement?'

She sighed. 'I suppose so. If I don't you'll just keep on and on at me.'

'Good.' He sounded genuinely pleased. 'At last you're doing something sensible.'

Her blue eyes regarded him doubtfully. 'That remains to be seen, doesn't it? I'm not into the business of counting chickens before they're hatched.'

He reached for her hand and drew her closer. 'You realise that this will make us partners in a way?'

'Yes. I...I suppose it will.' Why was she feeling a little breathless and why was her heart knocking so loud? And why was she asking herself stupid questions when she knew the answer perfectly well? It always happened when she looked into the depths of those grey eyes. They made her lose her senses.

'Then you and I must celebrate,' he said softly.

'M...must we?' His fingers were lightly caressing the nape of her neck, sending tremors down her spine. 'Wh...what did you have in mind?'

'Oh, I'll think of something.' He cupped her face in his hands and kissed the tip of her nose playfully, then he straightened up. 'Now let's get all this over and done with so that we can get out of here. I hate lawyers' offices.'

Half an hour later when they were out in the busy, sunlit street she glanced at her watch and said tentatively, 'We could go for a meal. Then I'll have to leave and start home. It's a long drive and I can't leave it too late.'

He looked down at her sternly. 'You're not going home tonight.' It was a flat statement that invited argument at her peril. 'You and I are going to spend a couple of days here, relaxing and enjoying each other's company.'

Uncertainty put a slight tremor in her voice. 'Th...that's not possible. I...I can't. I have to——'

He ignored her feeble protest and said briskly, 'I phoned Morag at midday to see if you'd left. She told me that you'd brought a change of clothes because you might decide to stay overnight, so don't argue with me. We'll collect them now. Where's your car?'

She told him and a few minutes later he'd retrieved her case from the Land Rover and she stood by helplessly as he hailed a passing taxi. Along with a ten-pound note he gave the driver instructions. 'Take this case to the Caledonian Hotel and hand it in at the reception desk. Tell them that Mr MacAllister will be in later to pick it up.'

Once the taxi had sped off Dirk nodded in satisfaction then said, 'Right. It's too early for a meal. We'll have a snack in the gardens meantime. We'll go to the hotel around six. You can freshen up and change, then we'll have dinner. After that...do you like Gilbert and Sullivan?'

Almost dazed by the speed of everything, she managed a nod.

'Good. I've got two tickets for *The Pirates of Penzance* at the King's Theatre. Then later on we'll take in a nightclub or disco or——'

'About the hotel,' she said quickly. 'I suppose you've already booked the rooms?'

'Room,' he corrected firmly.

Well, that answered the main question. 'Oh...I see.' She ran her tongue nervously over her lips, knowing that this was going to be the critical point of the day.

'Is there a problem?' His eyes, suddenly hard and uncompromising, were searching her face, demanding an immediate answer.

With a tightening of her throat and a sudden feeling of limb-weakening excitement she made her decision. 'No, Dirk. No problem at all.'

He gave a slow smile of satisfaction. 'Good. That's as it should be. This is Edinburgh, neutral ground to Highlanders like us. Perhaps here we can find peace. In Kinvaig we're victims. There's too much emotion and bitter memories. Here we can at least pretend for a while that the slate is clean.'

Unconvinced but uncaring, she nodded. 'We can pretend, yes. There's no harm in that, is there?'

Oblivious to the passing traffic and the people crowding and jostling them on the pavement he pulled her tightly against his chest and gave her a lingering and provocative kiss that left her trembling in her shoes. Withdrawing his mouth from hers, he lanced her mercilessly with his eyes and laid claim to her bare soul. 'We both know what we really want, don't we, Shona?'

A denial would have been hypocritical and foolish. A part of her mind had always known that this moment was inevitable. Ever since that night at his house she'd been fighting a rearguard action. He'd told her then that hunger was a more powerful motivator than family honour or pride, and he was right. For too many cold and lonely nights she'd hungered and ached. It was time her conscience went into cold storage for a change.

'Th...there's a busload of goggle-eyed strangers watching us,' she pointed out in breathless embarrassment. 'Can we start walking, please? I know that you never give a fig about what people think, but I don't like making an exhibition of myself.'

'You're blushing!' he observed, the sudden grin softening the hard angles of his features. 'Like a naughty little schoolgirl.'

'You're giving me plenty of reason to blush,' she told him primly. 'The middle of an Edinburgh street is no place to be carrying on like this.'

'Aye. You're right,' he teased good-naturedly. 'Civilisation does have its drawbacks.' He released her from his embrace. 'I've waited a long time. A few more hours won't make any difference. Come on. Let's grab a bite to eat.' Gallantly he offered her his arm, and together they made their way through St Andrew's Square towards Princes Street.

In the gardens they bought hamburgers, then he gestured up at the castle perched on its massive rock, the basaltic plug of a long-extinct volcano. 'No other city in the world can boast a sight like that. There's over a thousand years of history up there. But I often wonder why they built the damn thing so close to the railway station.'

It was the serious expression on his face as he said it that broke her up, and she almost choked over a crumb. When she got her breath back she gave him a reproving look. 'Don't come out with remarks like that while I'm eating.'

His easy smile was unrepentant. 'How well do you know Edinburgh?'

She gave a tiny shrug. 'I know the way from Queensferry to MacPhail's office and that's about all. I know Glasgow much better because I went to university there.'

'Then you're in luck. I went to Edinburgh University and I earned extra money during the holidays as a tourist guide.' He smiled wryly at the recollection. 'You wouldn't believe it. Japanese tourists wanting to know if there was a Yamamoto tartan. American millionaires wanting to know if Holyrood Palace was for sale because it sure would look nice back on their ranch in lil' ol' Texas.' He finished his hamburger then took her arm again enthusiastically. 'Did you know that Robert Louis Stevenson based his character of Dr Jekyll on an Edinburgh man? His name was Brodie and he was a deacon, an honest, upright churchman by day and a burglar and mugger by night. I'll show you the tavern where he and his cronies used to drink.'

During the next two hours she learnt more about the backstairs of Edinburgh's murky and violent past than would ever be written in a guidebook, but the real eye-opener was what she discovered about Dirk himself. He was a hard and fearless man, sometimes as quick to anger as herself. But she'd always known that. Now, for the first time, she was seeing the other side of him—a considerate and amiable companion with a razor-sharp wit and sense of humour.

At the end of the whirlwind tour they took a taxi to the West End hotel, and as he led her nonchalantly past the doorman into the busy lobby she felt a momentary feeling of nervousness.

Dirk collected her case from the reception desk, and when they made for the lift she wondered if her carefully contrived air of cool detachment was fooling anyone, or did she actually look as guilty as she felt? He'd probably signed them in as Mr and Mrs Smith. It was just the kind of to-hell-with-them-all thing he would do. In her mind's eye she could see the staff at the reception desk watching her every step with suspicion. Any moment now someone would lay a hand on her shoulder and say, 'I'm sorry, madam, but this is a respectable hotel. We don't allow that sort of thing here.' She should have bought a ring, something cheap...just for show. She should have——

'What's wrong?' asked Dirk, frowning at her in the lift. 'Are you feeling all right?'

She almost jumped with nervousness, then snapped, 'Of course I'm all right. Why shouldn't I be all right?'

He raised a hand. 'Don't bite my head off.'

She bit her lip in contrition then smiled. 'I...I'm sorry. I didn't mean to.'

The lift drew to a smooth halt and as they stepped out into the corridor he looked at her sharply. 'You're not having second thoughts about this, are you?'

'Of course not.' She bit her lip again then whispered fiercely, 'It's just that I'm not used to this kind of thing.'

'I know you're not,' he replied with dry amusement. 'If I thought for one moment that you were you wouldn't be here.'

Strangely enough she felt an immediate sense of relief and relaxation once they were inside the room with the door shut firmly against the outside world. Not even the sight of the large double bed worried her as she glanced around the well appointed room in approval. Thankfully she kicked off her shoes and curled her toes in the deep-pile of the carpet.

Dirk picked up the phone and she heard him ask for a dinner menu to be sent up.

She quickly unpacked her suitcase then said, 'I'm going to have a shower.'

He pointed. 'It's through there.' Then he grinned. 'Perhaps we should do our bit for ecology. We can save energy if we shower together. No? Oh, well, it was just an idea.'

Ten minutes later she emerged from the bathroom, pink and glowing and wrapped in one of the hotel's luxury bathrobes. 'It's your turn now. That'll give me a chance to get changed.'

He was sitting in the armchair and he looked up at her with a faintly mocking smile. 'You're acting very coy, Shona. Since we're going to be spending the night together I don't see what you're so——'

'This isn't tonight,' she said firmly. 'This is now, and I prefer privacy. You'll just have to wait.'

Uncoiling himself from the chair, he allowed his grey eyes to linger on her, then he sighed. 'OK. But somehow I have a feeling that my mind isn't going to be on Gilbert and Sullivan this evening.'

He displayed no such false modesty when he had finished his shower. She'd changed into a white silk blouse and dove-grey suit and was applying a touch of make-up at the dressing-table when she caught sight of him in the mirror. As naked as the day he was born, he wandered into the room, towelling vigorously at his dark hair, then strolled over to the wardrobe and selected his evening wear.

Over his shoulder he called to her, 'I took the liberty of ordering duck *à l'orange*. Is that all right with you?'

Quickly she averted her eyes from the reflection of his hard, lithe body in the mirror and cleared her throat. 'Yes. That sounds nice.' Blotting her lipstick on a napkin, she thought that he wasn't the only one who was going to have trouble concentrating this evening.

The dinner was mouth-wateringly gorgeous. So, for that matter, was Dirk. From the covert and envious glances of the other women diners she knew exactly what was going through their minds.

Never had his charismatic aura of masculine power and sexual attraction been so evident as it was this evening. He was dressed casually enough in a light-weight lounge suit much the same colour as her own, with a dark blue silk shirt and brightly coloured tie. But it was the suggestion of hard muscle and sinew beneath those clothes, the breadth of shoulder and slim hips, the raven-dark hair and the inner light behind those clear grey eyes that set him apart from other men. The knowledge that she was going to spend the night in his arms was making her dry-mouthed with excitement.

During the meal they'd engaged in casual small talk about the problems common to all Highland land-owners, but she got the impression that his mind was elsewhere. Finally, over the coffee, she said quietly, 'I want to apologise to you for the things I said in MacPhail's office, Dirk. It's just that . . . well, it was such a surprise when you turned up.'

For some reason the remark seemed to irritate him, and he gave her a brief nod. 'I've already told you. It was intentional. If you'd known that I was behind the offer you'd have suspected the worst. You've never trusted me, have you?'

It was a charge she could hardly deny, although it would have been easy enough to remind him of the reason for her mistrust. But then wasn't he the one who'd said that while they were here they could at least pretend that the slate was clean? They'd both made mistakes in the past, and he had no right to talk as if she alone were to blame.

Biting back on her resentment, she made an effort to smooth things over. 'What I'm trying to say, Dirk, is that I'm grateful for the way you're trying to help me keep the estate.'

His dark brows came together as he gave her a long, hard look, and she sensed the sudden drop in temperature. 'So you're grateful?' he remarked in a barbed voice. 'Is that why you're forcing yourself to face the distasteful task of sleeping with me tonight? A display of gratitude for saving you from ruin? Is this your idea of repaying a debt?'

The shock couldn't have been more electrifying if he'd slapped her across the face, and for a moment she sat in stunned silence. Then her fists slowly clenched and the blood pounded in her temples.

It was only the inhibiting effect of the genteel and elegant surroundings which prevented her from dashing her coffee in his face. Instead, she gathered up her handbag and got to her feet. Looking down at him, she said in a voice of blistering contempt, 'Goodnight, Mr MacAllister. You can send my half of the bill to me by post.'

Erect and dignified, she marched out of the dining-room, and continued through the hotel lobby and out into the street, where the doorman obligingly whistled up a taxi from the nearby rank.

CHAPTER EIGHT

IN THE back seat of the cab Shona's hand trembled as she searched hastily through her handbag for the keys to the Land Rover. Her case, with the rest of her clothes, was still in the hotel room, but she didn't care if she never saw them again. Right now she didn't care about anything except getting as far away as quickly as possible from that...that cretin.

She didn't know which was worse—her feeling of sick frustration or her outrage. How could he have thought such a thing, far less put it into words? He'd taken a simple expression of thanks and twisted it into something that sounded cheap and demeaning. But why? What cause had she given him? For the first time in years she'd really been enjoying herself. In spite of everything that had gone before she'd been prepared to forgive and forget, and there had seemed to be the chance of a real reconciliation. And then in a few short words of bitter accusation he'd brought her back to earth with a vengeance.

Could it have been a deliberate provocation? she wondered. He must have known that she'd never stand for an insult like that. Perhaps this was his twisted way of getting his revenge on her for having spurned him for so long. Anything was possible with a man like that.

The evening traffic had congested the streets, and she glanced at her watch impatiently. It had just gone seven, which meant that she wouldn't arrive home till after midnight, and the prospect of negotiating the narrow Highland roads in the dark was something she wasn't looking forward to. It would probably be a better idea to stop at Perth for the night. The Salutation was a comfortable hotel she'd used before. She could be there by nine, have an early night, then make an early start in the morning.

Gloomily she stared out of the taxi window, her eyes dull with pain and her heart heavy. One thing was for sure: hell would freeze over before she'd ever let MacAllister come within a mile of her again. This was the second time he'd made a fool of her. There wouldn't be a third. She'd see to that.

The taxi finally made it to St James's and after paying the driver she scorned the lift and took the stairs to the third level of the multi-storey. Her heels made a hollow, clicking sound on the concrete as she walked quickly towards the bay where the Land Rover was parked, and she'd almost reached it when the hand on her shoulder drew her up short and spun her around.

'Not so fast!'

Cold anger glinted at her through those grey eyes, and she drew in her breath. Damn him! He must have come out of the hotel after her and followed right behind in another taxi. Vigorously she shook herself free from his grip. 'I've got nothing to say to you, MacAllister. Go away and leave me alone.'

'I've got plenty to say to you,' he snapped. Before she knew what was happening he'd snatched the keys from her hand. 'You and I had an arrangement. We were going to spend the night together.'

'Give me those keys back,' she warned him quietly.

He slipped them into his pocket then grabbed her arm and grated, 'You're acting like a hot-headed little fool as usual. You're coming back to the hotel so that we can sort this mess out.'

'You're the one who's in a mess,' she fumed. 'If you don't give me those keys back right now I'm going to get the police and have you charged with——'

Her words were choked off as he kissed her with a savage hunger. The bruising onslaught of his lips took her breath away and as he kept his mouth clamped over hers her head began to swim. When at long last he decided to release her she remained exhausted in his arms, panting for breath, until she could finally summon enough strength to push him away. 'Theft! And now assault!' she gasped. 'You're in big trouble now, MacAllister.' Desperately she looked around the deserted parking area. 'I just hope there were witnesses to that.'

'There weren't,' he growled menacingly. 'Now, are you coming peacefully or will I have to drag you back?'

Suddenly nervous, she backed away. She had no doubt he'd carry out the threat. He certainly looked angry enough. He'd sling her over his shoulder, kicking and screaming, and march with her the length of Princes Street if he had to.

Taking a deep breath, she measured him with cold disdain. 'That's the only way you'll ever get anything from me, MacAllister. Brute force. But then that's your forte, isn't it?'

'At least it would be more honest,' he retorted. 'A damn sight more honest than you offering me your charms because you feel you're under some sort of obligation. But I really don't care one way or the other now.' He reached for her arm again. 'Now let's go. And don't give me any more——'

She shook him off once more. 'You've done it again!' she challenged bitterly. 'Insults! Do you think I'm the kind of woman who'd hop into bed with any man who'd done her a favour? What am I? Some sort of tramp?'

Her outburst brought a puzzled frown to his brow, then he asked quietly, 'Well, if gratitude isn't your reason, what is? I'm not foolish enough to imagine that you've suddenly fallen in love with me.'

She compressed her lips and eyed him with hot resentment. What kind of question was that to ask a woman? she thought. How could you possibly answer and still retain your sense of dignity? Finally, unable to contain herself any longer, she berated him soundly, 'Are you so unfeeling and thick-headed that I have to spell it out for you? I said that I'd sleep with you because I wanted to, dammit.' She glared at him a moment longer then looked away. 'Now I'm not so sure. I was beginning to change my mind about you, but it looks as if I was right the first time. Underneath all that humour and charm you're still the same old Dirk MacAllister intent on making a fool out of me.'

'Why did you act so reluctant when we first arrived at the hotel?' he demanded harshly. 'I've seen more enthusiasm in Mrs Ross faced with a week's ironing. You certainly weren't that passionless and apathetic that day on Para Mhor.'

It dawned on her slowly what he was driving at, and her cheeks coloured. 'That was five years ago, for heaven's sake! You think I was reluctant just because I didn't want to parade around naked in that hotel room the way you did?'

'That's right,' he asserted. 'Your body is nothing to be ashamed of. I've already seen it, remember?'

She swallowed. 'Yes. Only too well.' A feeling of unreality gripped her. 'Is that what this is all about, Dirk? Just because I didn't ... You thought that ... ?' She shook her head in disbelief at his misinterpretation of her actions. 'Look...' she said weakly. 'I...I was twenty when you first made love to me. I...wasn't scared of you then. You were like ... like something out of a dream. I was completely under your spell, a foolish young virgin wanting her first taste of life.'

She didn't object this time when he took her in his arms, but it was his turn to look distraught. 'Shona ... ? Are you telling me that you're frightened of me?'

She gave a meek nod of admission. 'Yes. Just a little. But to tell the truth I think I'm more frightened of myself. I should never have agreed to stay in the first place, but I ... I was too weak-willed to refuse. I don't know what your love life has been like during the last five years, but I've never allowed any man to use me the way you did.' She bit her lip in an agony of embarrassment at having to bare her soul and put her innermost, darkest secrets into words. She went on brokenly, 'I ... I've hated you all those years and ... and yet ...'

'Yet what?' he asked, softly cajoling the answer from her lips.

She gulped. 'Never mind. Let's just think of me as a textbook case of split personality.'

He held her in a warm and tender embrace for a moment, then he took the Land Rover keys from his pocket. 'Do you still want these?' he asked quietly. 'Or should we give ourselves another chance?'

She took the keys from him, then dumped them back in her handbag. 'About Gilbert and Sullivan . . .'

Before she had time to finish he took the tickets from his pocket and tore them in two, then grinned. 'I don't think we'll bother.'

The muted sound of the early morning traffic buzzed in her ears, and slowly she opened her eyes and yawned. Beside her, Dirk moved restlessly, although his breathing was deep and regular. Feeling drowsy and deliciously sensual, she put her arm around him and snuggled closer to the warmth of his body. Gently she traced her finger down the smooth skin of his chest, down further to the flat, hard muscles of his ridged stomach, then she stopped. It wouldn't be fair to waken him so early. The poor man must be exhausted after last night, and he surely deserved his rest. Anyway, it was still early. Later . . . three or four hours from now . . . She could wait. She brushed her lips gently over his bare shoulder in sweet anticipation.

He was the only lover she'd ever had, so she had no standard against which to compare him, but it was simply inconceivable that anyone could have been better. Last night as soon as they'd arrived back at the hotel their impatience to feed their mutual hunger for each other had been curbed only by his self-control, and it had been no blind, fumbling rush of frenzied passion. He had taken his time, with a sweet and unbearably tender build-up, his hands and mouth teasing her to an incandescent peak before the final, shattering climax of their union.

Afterwards they'd lain in each other's arms, both sated for the time being, content just to marvel and revel in the feelings of shared intimacy.

Later she'd gone for a shower and this time, as if to prove herself, she'd invited him to join her, and they'd laughed and cavorted like a couple of carefree children. They'd dried each other off, then he'd picked her up and carried her back to bed. As she'd lain, ready to accept him once more, he'd padded softly across the room to switch off the light and pull back the curtains. Suddenly her smooth, curvaceous form had been bathed in the soft glow of moonlight, and she'd closed her eyes in ecstatic pleasure as once again he'd begun the slow, sensual preliminaries towards complete possession.

It was nine o'clock when she awoke again, and this time Dirk rolled towards her and muttered sleepily, 'Roseanne? Is that you?'

She pinched his bare thigh between her finger and thumb and murmured, 'Yes. Is that you, Peter?'

He opened one eye. 'Who the hell is Peter?'

'Who the hell is Roseanne?'

He grinned. 'Never heard of her.' He sat up and stretched his arms and shoulders lazily, then looked down at her. 'We should get up for breakfast. Aren't you hungry?'

She reached up and traced her forefinger down his side then murmured, 'Very, very, very hungry.' Then her hand stole under the bedclothes on a journey of intimate exploration and her eyes widened and she gave an impish grin. 'And I'm not the only one, am I?'

With a groan and a sigh of pleasure he lay down again and reached for her.

Eventually they were too late for breakfast and made do with coffee sent up by Room Service.

'I'll show you more of Edinburgh today,' he offered. 'Unless there's something else you'd rather do. We could go through to Glasgow if you'd prefer and look up some of your old student haunts.'

She frowned and laid down her cup. 'Actually I'd intended going home today.' She saw the quick tightening of his mouth then added, 'But I suppose I could put it off till tomorrow, couldn't I?'

'Yes. I suggest you do that.' He leaned back in his chair and eyed her sternly. 'Kinvaig can get on without you and me for a while yet.' A faintly mocking smile appeared briefly on his lips. 'After all, one night isn't enough to make up for five years, is it?'

She finished her coffee and as he obligingly poured her another cup he said, 'Right now it's our future I want to discuss, Shona.'

'Our... our future?'

'Aye. You and I together for the rest of our lives. Marriage. I won't let you down this time, I promise.'

She bit her lip and lowered her eyes. 'I... I was afraid that this was going to happen. Can't we discuss it some other time? Everything has been so wonderful. Let's not spoil it by arguing, Dirk.' It was a plea of desperation. They'd both shared something beautiful... an experience she'd always treasure... but now it was all in danger of turning into cold ashes.

He stiffened in his chair and asked her bluntly, 'Does that mean that you don't want to marry me?'

'I'm saying that I can't marry you.' Her voice was dull and pain-racked. 'There's a big difference.'

He weighed her answer carefully then caused her to flinch by the hard and bitter accusation in his voice.

'Well, I know that there isn't anyone else in your life, so that can only mean one thing. You still haven't forgiven me for the past, have you?'

As she shook her head she could feel the misery welling up in her. 'It . . . it isn't that, Dirk. I know you better now and I know the kind of man you really are. You must have had a very good reason for not turning up to meet my father. I can accept that now.'

His brows came together in a dark frown. 'Then what?' he demanded.

She balked at the question. 'I . . . I'd rather not tell you. I've hurt you enough.'

'Aye . . .' he agreed harshly. 'You have hurt me. But I'm afraid I'm going to have to insist that you tell me. If I'm to be burdened with the blame for something I've a right to know what it is.'

Accepting the justification of his argument, she took a deep breath and fought to keep her voice from trembling. 'We . . . we're both to blame. Me as much as you.'

'Go on,' he urged. 'Blame for what?'

'The death of my father. When he knew that I wanted to marry you it . . . it broke his heart. He was never the same from that day until the day he died.' She shook her head in despair at the memory. 'The idea of his daughter wanting to marry a MacAllister destroyed him. That's why I can't marry you, Dirk. That shadow would always come between us. In the end it would kill our marriage.'

The colour drained from his face and he stared at her in bleak silence. Finally he sighed heavily. 'Aye. It's the curse of our Celtic souls. We always have to be placating the ghosts of our ancestors.'

'It . . . it's just the way I am, Dirk.'

'Do you really believe that was what he died from?' he asked coldly. 'I was led to believe it was heart failure.'

'You weren't there,' she said bitterly. 'You didn't have to watch him fading away before your eyes.'

He rose from the table and went over to the window. For a while he stared thoughtfully down at the West End traffic having its usual mid-morning snarl-up, then he turned and said quietly, 'The ghost of my own father also has to be placated, Shona. I can't be the last of the line. I need an heir. The estate will have to be passed on some day.'

'Yes, Dirk,' she replied with quiet resignation, wishing he would change the subject. 'I can understand that.'

'Then understand this,' he said grimly. 'If you won't marry me I'll go out and find someone who will. I'll do it out of necessity, not out of love or loneliness. She can be plain or beautiful. It won't matter to me.'

She listened to him in a stricken silence. Last week she wouldn't have given a damn what he did. But after last night? Why had she let last night happen? She should have foreseen this. Instead she'd acted like a fool and let her own blind desire lead them both into this mess. She'd been willing enough to accept his lovemaking, knowing that if he offered his heart she would turn him away. She was nothing more than a cruel, callous bitch.

'I . . . I'm sorry, Dirk. I really am.' She was too dejected and disgusted with herself to say anything else.

'So am I,' he remarked sourly. 'And we'll both be sorrier. It means that some day I'm going to bring a stranger to Kinvaig. That stranger will be my wife and she'll bear my children. I'll be a good husband to her and I'll do everything I can to give her a good life. But my love will only be a pretence. You're the one I'll always truly love.'

She wished that she could close her ears, but he went on, every word stabbing deeper and deeper into her heart.

'You and I will still be neighbours,' he reminded her grimly. 'As a new member of the community my wife will want to meet you. That's something that can't be avoided without raising suspicion. But if I tell her that you and I were once lovers she'll always feel vulnerable. That's human nature.'

She swallowed a painful lump in her throat. 'Then don't tell her. I certainly won't.'

'Aye. That sounds easy until you think about it. Once I'm a married man we're off limits to one another. Neither you nor I would tolerate a clandestine affair. But our feelings for one another won't just disappear. Love isn't a coat you can put on or take off according to the weather. Then again she might find out the truth. There's already gossip about us in Kinvaig. Sooner or later she'd be bound to hear it. Or can you imagine me making love to her and pretending it's you? They say a woman can always tell. It wouldn't be fair on her and it would be an impossible situation for you and me. Our lives wouldn't be worth living. Is it worth going through all that because of a father who's dead and buried?'

'You know the answer to that as well as I do,' she whispered brokenly. 'He may be dead, but I couldn't... couldn't... Damn you, Dirk! Can't you understand? Rory may have had his faults, but he was my father and I loved him.'

'Aye,' he muttered. 'I know that only too well. And that's what's causing all this trouble.' He paused then added enigmatically, 'Rory would have had a lot of explaining to do when he finally met his maker.'

She gave him a sharp look. 'What do you mean by that?'

'Nothing,' he growled impatiently. 'Forget it.'

She got to her feet, anger bringing life back into her eyes. 'I won't forget it! Just what exactly are you getting at? What is it that my father would have to explain?'

For a moment it looked as if he was going to tell her, then he changed his mind and said drily, 'At least you were right when you said that he didn't want me as a son-in-law. Well, he seems to have got his way in the end, so we'll just let the old fox rest in peace, shall we?'

Old fox? Suddenly she remembered Morag describing her father as a sly old devil, and Lachie had called him ruthless. It was as if they all knew something about Rory that they were reluctant to tell her. But surely she had known him better than any of them? After all, they'd been father and daughter, with no secrets from one another. Or had they?

She might have left it at that had her frustration not got the better of her. 'Look, Dirk. You're making veiled accusations about a man you hardly knew. You never really met or had much to do with him, did you? You're only going by hearsay—things your own father probably told you. That's not being very fair to him, is it?'

Her denunciation brought an ironic twist to his lips. 'Then why not level the same charge at Rory? What did he really know about me apart from the fact that I was the son of his worst enemy? Not a thing. I was a MacAllister, and that was enough for him. Would you call that fair?'

There had to be an answer to that if only she could think of it, but she couldn't.

The silence between them grew heavy and at last he shrugged. 'I don't suppose there's much point in either of us staying here now.'

Their eyes met. In his she saw anger, regret and a stark challenge, and she knew that this was her last chance. This was where the road branched. Either they continued down it together or they went their separate ways. Then in the mist of her hesitation and torn emotions the spirit of her father seemed to beckon, and she lowered her eyes. 'I'm sorry, Dirk. I . . . I'll start packing my case.'

An hour later she was in the Land Rover crossing the Forth Bridge and heading through Fife.

At Pitlochry, where the rolling hills of Perthshire met the fringes of the massive Cairngorms, she pulled into a lay-by and cut the engine. It was too hard to concentrate on her driving for any length of time. Thoughts and questions kept churning through her mind, and she wondered if her refusal to marry Dirk was a mistake she'd regret for the rest of her life. Ahead of her the northern sky looked dark and threatening, but it was too late to turn back now. With her finger she angrily brushed a tear from the corner of her eye.

CHAPTER NINE

SHONA would have preferred a few days of peace and tranquillity to lick her wounds, get her emotions under control, and start making some sort of plan for the future, but she'd rightly suspected that she wouldn't get a chance.

No sooner had she parked the Land Rover and walked into the kitchen than Morag launched into her own special brand of interrogation. 'Well? What did your lawyer want to see you about that was so important?'

She helped herself to tea and a piece of home-made cake. 'Estate business, Morag. Nothing that would really interest you.' It was an airy, innocent-sounding response designed to stop Morag in her tracks, but it didn't.

'Huh! It's like that, is it?' Morag made her displeasure clear by pummelling the dough for next day's bread with exaggerated vigour. 'I'm not a part of the estate, then? Born here in this very house in your grandfather's time. Grew up here and took over from my mother as housekeeper when she retired. Practically brought you up with precious little help from your father when your own mother died. Cleaned, cooked, scrubbed...'

Shona looked heavenwards then sighed, 'All right, Morag. I'm sorry. You're right. You have as much right to know what's going on as anyone else.'

Morag sniffed. 'Aye. I should think so.'

'It was an advertising firm,' Shona explained patiently. 'They want to use the name and a picture of Glen Gallan in an advertising campaign. MacPhail seems to think it'll draw the tourists here and put the estate back in business.'

Morag gave the dough a well earned rest and frowned. 'That sounds like good news. I can't imagine why you weren't bursting to tell me as soon as you came in instead of trying to keep it a secret.'

'I'd rather wait and see if the tourists really do come,' she answered cautiously. 'If they do, then it'll be time enough to celebrate.'

'Aye,' muttered Morag, her native shrewdness appreciating such caution. She attacked the dough again. 'And what did Dirk MacAllister have to do with it?'

'MacAllister?' She raised an innocent eyebrow.

Morag gave her a sidelong, sarcastic look. 'He was there, wasn't he?'

Shona sighed in exasperation. 'How did you know?'

'Because he phoned up at lunchtime yesterday to ask if you'd left in time for the meeting.'

Dammit! She'd forgotten all about that. Well, she hadn't wanted to get into a discussion about Dirk, but now it seemed she had no choice. Morag would just keep digging away until she knew everything.

She rose from the table and poured herself another cup of tea from the pot on the Aga. 'Dirk was there because it's his whisky they want to advertise. They want to call it "Glen Gallan".'

Morag's eyes widened in surprise. 'A Struan helping a MacAllister! I never thought I'd live to see the day.'

She gave a shrug. 'I don't see any harm in it. I've got nothing to lose, and, if it puts money into the estate, all the better.'

Morag smiled broadly for the first time in years. 'Well, I'm glad to see that you're getting some sense at last.'

Shona took exception to that and said tartly, 'I'm not a fool. No one in their right mind would have turned down a deal like that.'

'Your father would have,' Morag asserted firmly. 'He'd never have got himself involved in anything to do with the MacAllisters.'

'Well, I'm not my father. I've got a mind of my own.'

'Aye. Thank God for that, or we'd all be in the poorhouse shortly,' Morag said fervently. 'Thick-headedness doesn't run in the family after all. There's hope yet.'

It was the first time she'd ever heard Morag speak with such deliberate disrespect about her father, and she gave her a sharp, quizzical look. It was high time Morag started answering a few questions instead of asking them.

'So I suppose you and Dirk spent the night together in Edinburgh?' Morag went on unsparingly.

Shona tightened her lips. 'Now that is personal, Morag. It really is none of your business.'

Morag nodded in understanding. 'Well, that means that you did, otherwise you'd have denied it right away.' She smiled again. 'Anyway, when you didn't come home last night I phoned Mrs Ross. Dirk wasn't home either.'

'So you just put two and two together, is that it?'

'Aye. I'm good at that,' Morag admitted drily. 'I get plenty of practice at it in this house.'

'All right,' Shona conceded. 'Dirk and I spent the night at the Caledonian Hotel in Edinburgh. Now I suppose it'll be all over Kinvaig by tomorrow.'

'I don't gossip,' Morag said severely. 'I might listen to it, but I don't go around spreading it.' She gave the dough a final wallop. 'Anyway, it's the best news I've heard in a long time. This stupidity has gone on for far too long. I'm glad it's over and that the pair of you have made up.'

Shona kept her mouth shut and Morag looked at her with sudden suspicion. 'It is over, isn't it?'

Suddenly all the misery she'd been suppressing on the long drive home welled up and lodged in her throat, and she said in a broken whisper, 'I . . . I don't want to talk about it, Morag.'

'I see.' Morag cleaned and dried her hands at the sink. 'So you'd rather keep it all to yourself, would you? Don't you think it would be more sensible to get it off your chest? You've confided in me before. Why not now?'

'You . . . you wouldn't understand how I feel.'

Morag put her arm gently around her shoulder in a gesture of affection. 'Maybe I wouldn't. But I can recognise a broken heart when I see one. Now sit down at the table and tell me all about it. If Dirk MacAllister just used you then cast you aside I'll have a few words to say to him.'

'No. You've got it wrong, Morag. It . . . it was the other way round. I love him, Morag, but I told him that I wouldn't marry him.'

'So you still haven't forgiven him for what he did all those years ago? Is that it?'

She swallowed painfully. 'Not just that. I . . . I'd be betraying my father.'

Morag stiffened then echoed in disbelief. 'Betraying your father! Are you mad, lassie? He's dead and gone. Forget about him.'

She looked at the housekeeper in horror. 'Forget about him? That's a terrible thing to say! I loved him. I'll never forget him.'

'Aye. You loved him all right,' Morag said bitterly. 'It's just a pity that he never loved you back half as much.'

'You...you don't know what you're talking about,' Shona said, aghast at the accusation.

Morag went on adamantly, 'Rory Struan had a heart of stone. Never once did he take you on his knee when you were a bairn. Never once did he give you a kiss or a cuddle. And as for your poor mother—he never forgave her for dying before she could give him the son he really wanted. That's the kind of man your precious father was.'

Shona sprang to her feet, knocking over her chair, and snapped, 'Just remember who you are, Morag. You're stepping over the line when you dare talk to me like that about my father.'

'Why not?' asked Morag quietly. 'Are you frightened of the truth? It gives me no pleasure to speak ill of the dead, but I'll not see him reach out from the grave and destroy your only chance of happiness.'

'I couldn't have put it better myself,' drawled the voice from the doorway.

They both turned in surprise. Being too involved in their argument, neither of them had heard Dirk's car arrive, nor the kitchen door open as he let himself in.

Morag got to her feet awkwardly. 'Aye... Well, I'll leave you two to sort things out by yourselves.'

Dirk raised a restraining hand. 'I'd rather you stayed, Morag. I need all the allies I can get.'

Morag smiled. 'As you like. You'll take a wee dram?'

'No, thanks. Tea will be fine.'

Shona had got over her initial surprise at seeing him and now she gave a tentative smile. 'I...I thought you'd be staying in Edinburgh for a while.'

'Looking for someone to marry?' he asked ironically. 'Would you rather I had?'

He turned his attention to Morag. 'You were doing a pretty good job of character assassination just now. Is there anything else you'd care to tell Shona about her father?' His tone was neutral, making it hard to decide whether he approved or disapproved.

Morag seemed to be beyond caring one way or the other and she retorted, 'There's plenty I could tell. You might call it disloyalty, but it's time Shona knew the truth. Aye...and I've a feeling there's a few things you could be telling. It's only a case of sparing her feelings that's stopped you so far, isn't it?'

Shona's eyes darted from one to the other, then she demanded, 'What things? What's this big secret everyone is keeping from me?'

Dirk sighed heavily. 'Dammit, Shona. I thought that I was ready for this, but it's harder than I thought. It's too high a price...'

She looked at him blankly and Morag explained his dilemma. 'He knows that you loved your father, but the only way he can get you to marry him is by destroying that love.' She confronted Dirk. 'Aren't you at least going to tell her about the night Rory visited you? She still thinks you changed your mind at the last minute and ran out on her.'

Dirk looked at her sharply. 'Who told you about that night?'

Morag smiled with quiet satisfaction. 'You did. Just now. When you didn't deny it. Mind you, I'd always suspected it. When I saw him leave the house that night——'

'What night?' asked Shona, getting more bewildered and shocked by the minute.

'It was the day you and Dirk had been to Para Mhor,' Morag recalled. 'Rory had been away to the auction at Inverness and he came home about ten that night. You were in the library. I heard him shouting at you and I guessed you'd told him about being out with Dirk. I went to bed soon after that, but I couldn't sleep. Then about two in the morning I heard the car engine start up. I got up and looked out of my window in time to see Rory drive away.' She paused and looked at Dirk. 'He was gone about two hours. I suppose the pair of you had a lot to talk about.'

'Aye, we did,' agreed Dirk with a growl. 'Though he did most of the talking and shouting.'

Morag nodded. 'I can imagine him and that black temper of his. Anyway, according to Mrs Ross you left the house about six in the morning——'

'I warned Mrs Ross to keep her mouth shut about Rory's visit,' Dirk said severely.

'She's never mentioned it to me,' said Morag in his housekeeper's defence, 'only about you leaving in the morning without an explanation. And no one saw hide nor hair of you until the day they buried Rory.'

Dirk nodded. 'That was part of the deal he made with me.'

Shona felt her stomach turning over and she looked at Dirk in stark disbelief. 'A deal? You deserted me as part of a deal?'

Dirk's face was grave. 'I had no choice. He didn't fight fair. He used emotional blackmail.' He spread his hands helplessly. 'He was in such a towering rage that he was threatening to kill you sooner than let you marry me.'

The colour drained from her face. 'You're lying. My own father...?'

Dirk went on relentlessly. 'I told him not to be so bloody stupid and to stop and think about what he was saying. Then he changed his mind. Instead of killing you he was going to disinherit you... disown you completely.'

'And... and that was enough to make you desert me?' she asked brokenly. 'If he disinherited me you wouldn't get your hands on the estate. That's what you were after all the time, wasn't it? You lied to me?' Suddenly, her eyes filling with tears of rage, she dashed past him and out of the kitchen. Only when she reached the beach did she stop her headlong flight, then she buried her face in her hands and sobbed in despair.

Gradually the pain subsided and raw emotion was replaced by rational thought. The accusation she'd flung at Dirk had been totally unjustified. She'd simply struck out in blind anger at the nearest target. Common sense told her that Morag and Dirk couldn't both be lying about her father. It was true, as Morag had said, that her father had never showed her any real affection, but in her childish ignorance she hadn't expected it. What you never had you never missed. Anyway, she hadn't needed affection. Rory had been an almost godlike creature in her young and innocent eyes. At school she'd been content to bask in the reflected glory of his reputation as a man to be feared and respected.

She heard the crunch of footsteps on the shingle behind her and slowly she turned to face Dirk.

He looked down into her face with compassion. 'You've been crying.'

'Yes . . .' she muttered. 'It . . . it doesn't matter. I'm all right now. I just had to let it out.'

With infinite tenderness he took her in his arms and kissed her closed eyes gently. 'I've hurt you, Shona. I never wanted you to find out. I'd have done anything to spare you this pain.'

She pressed her cheek against the warmth of his chest and listened to the heavy, tortured beat of his heart. Looking up, she smiled wanly. 'It's my own fault, Dirk. I left you with no option but to tell me. I wouldn't marry you because of . . . of him. If only I'd found out sooner.' Those grey eyes which had mocked and taunted her so often were now filled with anguish, and she said quietly, 'There's more, isn't there? You didn't leave just because he threatened to disown me, did you?'

'No, I didn't.' He studied her for a moment then shook his head doubtfully. 'This is going to hurt you even more. You'd be better off not knowing.'

She challenged his statement with a lift of her eyebrows. 'Would I? Do you expect me to live the rest of my life in ignorance, lying awake at night and wondering . . . my mind never at rest? Oh, no, Dirk. I'm not having that to look forward to. I want it all out in the open here and now. The sooner I know, then the sooner I'll come to terms with it.' She paused then added bitterly, 'I don't think I'll be shocked at anything you tell me about my father now. What worse thing could a father do to his daughter than disown her merely for falling in love with someone he didn't like?'

Dirk nodded and sighed as he reluctantly acknowledged her right to know the truth. 'You didn't realise that your father was an ill man on the night he came to see me, did you?'

She blinked in surprise. 'No. I could see that there was something wrong with him shortly after that, though.'

'Aye,' Dirk said angrily. 'It suited his purpose to let you think that you'd been the cause of his condition. But the fact is that he'd been ill for a long time.'

She frowned. 'Are you certain? Surely I'd have known. What was wrong with him?'

'His heart. He needed a bypass operation.' Dirk waited until that had sunk in, then he said grimly, 'He hadn't gone to an auction in Inverness that day. He'd gone to see a specialist and he was told that unless he had the operation the prognosis was bad. Two years at the most. He showed me the specialist's report.'

The news completely stunned Shona for a moment, then her voice quavered. 'Why didn't he have the operation if it was to save his life?'

Dirk shrugged. 'He hated the thought of surgery. He was convinced that the operation would kill him. He preferred to take the two-year option.'

She shook her head in disbelief at her father's stupidity. So he'd been afraid of at least one thing after all—the surgeon's knife. Well, everyone had their convictions and private nightmares.

Dirk went on, angrier than ever as he relived the night of the confrontation. 'Rory knew that I wasn't going to knuckle down to his threats and bluster, so he made me a deal. He wanted me to leave and have no further contact with you. It would only be for two years, he said. Perhaps only one. Then once he was dead you could do as you pleased. I could come back and marry you if you still wanted me.' He looked at her with an expression of helpless anger. 'What was I supposed to do? How could I turn down the request of a dying man? But just in case I did he had another card to play. Unless I agreed to his terms he said he'd sell Glen Gallan to an oil company.'

She stared at him in utter bewilderment. 'Why on earth would an oil company want to buy Glen Gallan?'

'Because, according to what your father told me, it's right on top of a vast oil deposit. It seems that one of the Army officers who trained there during the war was a mining engineer and geologist. He made a study of the area and told your grandfather.' His grey eyes studied her closely for a moment, watching her reaction, then he said quietly, 'You must know what Rory's threat meant to the whole area, including my own estate. Can you imagine this part of the country despoiled by oil derricks, pumping stations, oil tanks, pipelines? The risk of pollution over miles of coastline? There'd be no more tourists. No more fishing-boats. No more Kinvaig. It would be the end of a way of life for hundreds of people here.'

A shudder ran through her that her father could ever have contemplated such a thing. Then sudden understanding came to her and she eyed him shrewdly. 'That's why you always insisted that I should never sell out to a stranger. In case they found out about the oil?'

He nodded grimly. 'Other people might not have the feelings about this land that you and I share. They'd only be interested in the money they could make.'

Once again Shona felt sick. Swallowing back her bitterness, she cursed softly under her breath. 'He had the gall to accuse me of bringing the Struan name into disrepute and yet he was prepared to do a thing like that! Why couldn't he just have accepted the fact that we loved one another and left it at that?'

'Because you were a Struan and you wanted to marry a MacAllister, that's why,' Dirk answered, his anger now tempered to a cold condemnation. 'His pride and reputation meant more to him than the happiness of his own daughter.'

She had a sudden, vivid memory of that night so long ago. She'd been in the library when her father had returned from his trip to Inverness. He'd looked tired and worn. She'd poured him a drink and he'd become maudlin, telling her how proud he was of her and how much she reminded him of her mother and how she was the only thing left in the world that meant anything to him. At the time she'd felt slightly embarrassed at his unaccustomed words of affection, because they'd been so out of character. Now, of course, she knew the reason. The news from the specialist had shaken him and made him start to feel sorry for himself.

She pushed the memory aside and listened as Dirk went on, 'I had to wait four years until Rory's death released me from my promise. As soon as I got word I came back.'

'And I'd have nothing to do with you,' she reminded him with sad bitterness. 'All I could think of was the humiliation I'd suffered and the hurt I'd caused my father.'

He smiled thinly at the memory. 'I wasn't sure what kind of reception I was going to get, but I didn't expect to be threatened with a shotgun.'

She bit her lip and blushed at the memory, then said in exasperation, 'You should have told me there and then about my father.'

'On the very day of his funeral?' He eyed her sceptically. 'It was obvious you weren't going to listen to anything I said. You'd already made up your mind about me.'

He put his arm around her and they walked slowly back towards the house.

'Well, you should have told me about him when we were in Edinburgh,' she insisted. 'When I blamed you for his ill health ... That would have been the time. But you ... you made no attempt to defend yourself. Dammit, Dirk! You should have told me everything then.'

'Aye...' he reflected with bitter hindsight. 'I almost did. But when it came to the crunch I couldn't harden my heart enough.' He nodded towards the house. 'It's only thanks to Morag that I'm telling you now. When I arrived in the kitchen she was busy knocking your father off his pedestal. She started it, so I decided to finish it.'

The enormity of her father's deception and the way she'd fallen for it would take a long time to sink in, she realised. Because of him both she and Dirk had wasted five years of their lives—years which they could have shared together in love and happiness. And his motive had been family pride and honour, as Dirk had suggested? It hardly seemed possible.

They were drawing nearer the house now and suddenly her step faltered and a cold breeze stirred the fine hairs on the back of her neck. Dirk's arm tightened in support and he looked down at her in anxiety. 'What's wrong, Shona?'

'There!' She pointed a shaking finger towards the eaves of the house. 'Those windows! They look strange.'

He glanced up and frowned. 'It's nothing. Only the reflection of the light from the sea and sun.'

She stood for a moment longer, staring at the milky opacity of the glass. Yes, she thought. Reflection. That was what it must have been. But these were the windows of her father's bedroom, and for a moment they'd seemed to be glaring at her like a pair of malevolent eyes.

Even the strength and protection of Dirk's arm around her couldn't dispel the cold fear that permeated her body, and she shivered once more.

When they reached the kitchen Dirk helped her gently into a seat and gave a brisk nod to Morag. 'Some hot tea with plenty of sugar.'

Shona looked up at him in awkward embarrassment. 'I'm all right now. I . . . I don't know what came over me.'

Even his confident smile couldn't hide the concern in his eyes. 'You need a couple of days' rest, relaxing and taking things easy.' He turned to the housekeeper. 'Take good care of her, Morag. I'm depending on you. Phone me if anything——'

'You needn't tell me how to look after her,' Morag said stiffly. 'I've been doing it all my life.'

Dirk conceded the point with an apologetic nod. 'I know that you have. But this isn't anything physical. She's had an emotional shock and she's vulnerable. She'll get over it with a bit of tender, loving care. All I'm asking you to do is to keep a very special eye on her.' Bending down, he kissed Shona gently on the mouth then whispered, 'I'll come and see you in a couple of days.' Finally, with one last smile of sympathy, he straightened up and signalled Morag to follow him outside.

Shona lifted the cup from the table and sipped gratefully at the sweet tea. She wished she hadn't made such a fool of herself in front of Dirk. Those windows... It had been overwrought imagination, and she'd reacted like a frightened child.

A few moments later she heard the car drive off, then Morag came in and said briskly, 'I'll run a nice hot bath for you, then you can——'

'There's no need for that,' she said in a voice which had regained some of its former authority. 'I'm perfectly capable of running my own bath. Pay no attention to Dirk. He's making too much of a fuss over me.'

'So he is,' agreed Morag with a rare smile. 'You're lucky you have a man like him to make a fuss over you.' She poured herself a cup of tea then said cheerfully, 'I suppose we'd better start making plans for the wedding.'

Once more she felt that odd chill at the back of her neck, and she looked at Morag vaguely. 'Wedding?'

'Aye. Wedding,' repeated Morag, eyeing her with a puzzled expression. 'He told me that you'd both ironed out your differences. He seems to think that it's all settled now.'

With lips that had suddenly gone stiff and a throat that had gone unaccountably dry, she found herself evading a direct answer. 'I . . . I don't know what gave him that idea.' Taking a deep breath, she got to her feet then muttered, 'I . . . I'd rather not talk about it at the moment.'

Morag sighed in exasperation. 'Suit yourself. But Dirk MacAllister won't wait forever. I've a feeling that you're stretching the poor man's patience to the limit.'

CHAPTER TEN

THE throaty growl of the engine carried faintly across Glen Gallan on the still morning air, and Shona went out to the veranda of the chalet. Shading her eyes with her hand, she saw the Land Rover making its precarious descent from the high moor. At this distance it was hard to tell whose it was. It wouldn't be Lachie. She'd made sure that he and young Jamie had had plenty of work to keep them occupied elsewhere on the estate for the rest of the week. That left only one other possibility. It had to be Dirk.

Wearing a troubled frown, she went back inside. Morag was the only person who knew she was here, and she'd been sworn to secrecy, but Dirk had still managed to track her down. Well, the two days and nights she'd already spent here hadn't done her any good, because she still felt as miserable and confused as ever, so perhaps it was just as well that he'd turned up. A confrontation was inevitable, so the sooner she got it over with, the better.

She'd tidied away the breakfast dishes and was busy flicking dust from the furniture when she heard him climb the few steps of the veranda and walk into the room.

Feeling a bit sheepish, she greeted him with an awkward smile and said, 'I thought it was you coming. Sit down and I'll make some fresh coffee.'

He was wearing jeans and a leather jacket over a plain white T-shirt. Tall and wide-shouldered, he

172

somehow made the room seem smaller, and she tried to read the expression in his eyes. Was he disappointed... angry...?

He gave her a brief nod. 'Thanks. I could do with it.' With an easy nonchalance he lowered himself into a seat and took in his surroundings with approval. 'This is the first time I've been in one of your chalets. I'm impressed.'

She filled the coffee-pot and put it on the stove. 'I'm afraid we don't run to percolators yet. You'll have to have instant.'

He shrugged. 'A small price to pay for such charming surroundings.'

Was he being sarcastic? she wondered. 'I suppose Morag told you I was here.'

He shrugged. 'Morag isn't a good liar. She has neither the talent nor the desire. At first she tried to fob me off with some tale about you having gone to Inverness for a few days. Then she "inadvertently" let slip the fact that you'd loaded up the jeep with enough tinned food to last a week. No one takes tinned food to Inverness, do they?'

He smiled at her, but behind the pleasant manner his eyes were resentful, demanding an explanation for her behaviour.

Guiltily she avoided his penetrating gaze and swallowed nervously. 'I'm sorry for not telling you, Dirk. I... I just wanted to be on my own for a while. I needed time to think. And I... I had to get away from that house.'

He leaned forward. 'Aye... Morag told me you'd been acting strange. Not eating. Not sleeping. Hardly talking.'

She gave a helpless shrug. 'I felt . . . oppressed. It's hard to describe.'

'Oppressed by my attentions?' he asked roughly. 'Is that why you want to be on your own?'

Her voice wavered. 'N . . . no. Of course not.'

He studied her in cold silence for a moment then growled, 'You don't sound very convincing, Shona. If you want nothing more to do with me just say so now. I won't impose myself on you any longer.'

Suddenly all the misery that had been weighing her down for the last few days welled up inside her and a silent tear rolled down her cheek. 'Don't leave me, Dirk. Please stay. I . . . I need you. I . . . I think I must be losing my mind. I need to talk to you.'

Her breakdown brought him instantly to his feet and by her side. Taking her in his arms, he harshly snapped her out of her near-hysteria. 'All right, Shona! That's enough! There's nothing wrong with your mind. You're as sane as I am.'

'Am I?' Her blue eyes looked up at him, pleading. 'Then why am I feeling so guilty about wanting to marry you, darling? Why doesn't he leave me alone instead of tormenting me all the time?'

He cupped her face in his strong hands and smiled with satisfaction. 'So you really do want to marry me?'

'I've never wanted anything so much in my life,' she whispered. 'I'd die if you went off and married someone else.'

'That's all I wanted to hear,' he murmured in her ear. 'Nothing else matters.' His lips traced a path across her cheek until they found and covered her willing mouth. His kiss was suddenly hard and demanding, and the contact sent warm vibrations of love and desire through her slender, quivering body. Knowing the outcome, she began to respond, slowly at first, then with ever increasing urgency, as her fingers entwined themselves feverishly in his dark hair. The clean, masculine scent of him was invading her senses and heightening her awareness. Her body began to mould itself to his, feeling his warmth and his strength, absorbing and revelling in it. Inexorably her hunger began gnawing, demanding satisfaction.

. Dirk, instantly aware of her raging desire, swept her up into his arms and, still kissing her, carried her through to the bedroom.

She stood in utter abandonment as he undressed her slowly, his grey eyes reflecting his pleasure at each new revelation. Then they made love slowly and sweetly, each responding to the other's needs with an eagerness to please. His sensitive touch and the heat of his mouth sent rivers of fire through her flesh. When finally their bodies began to move together in deep, sensuous rhythm she closed her eyes and dug her fingers into his back until the storm of passion was over, leaving her gasping and filled with a wondrous feeling of contentment.

Dirk waited until her panting breath had returned to normal, then he rolled on to his side and pressed his lips to her damp brow. 'You've certainly proved one thing,' he whispered.

'What's that?' she murmured back dreamily.

He gave her a smile of infinite tenderness. 'That you've been missing me as much as I've been missing you.'

They lay side by side, gazing into each other's eyes, while the fingers of his right hand traced a quivering path up and down her naked spine.

'Can you smell something burning?' she asked, wrinkling her nose. Suddenly she sat up. 'My God! The coffee-pot! It'll be burnt through by now.'

Dirk leapt out of bed. 'I'll get it.'

She sat on the edge of the bed, gnawing at her lip, until he returned and put her mind at ease. 'The place won't burn down. I got to it in time.'

'Good.' She gazed up at his magnificent body, then slowly got to her feet and smiled at him knowingly. 'I feel like a shower. Care to join me?'

They were still wrapped in a feeling of warm, loving intimacy when they finally went out on to the veranda with their coffee. By now the sun was higher, dappling the Glen with the shadows of the small, fleecy white clouds. A herd of red deer grazed their way casually along the heather-covered flank of the hill to their right. The only sounds were the soft chuckle of the river and the occasional lonely cry of a curlew.

A feeling of sadness came over her, misting her blue eyes, and she sighed. 'I've always loved Glen Gallan. I wish I could stay here forever. I wish we both could. I don't want to go back to that house. I'll never feel comfortable there again.'

Dirk laid a comforting hand on her shoulder. 'I wish I could tell you otherwise, Shona, but I can't. It's not the house you're afraid of. It's the memories it contains. You've got to face up to him sooner or later. When you've done that, then you can start a new life with me.'

She looked at him with a blank expression. 'I ... I don't know what you're talking about. Face who?'

'Your father, of course. You know perfectly well what I'm talking about.'

The mild reprimand in his voice chastened her and she muttered, 'You ... you don't understand. No one could.'

'I understand that you're running away from him,' he said with resigned patience. 'Morag has told me how you've been acting in the house. You gathered up all his pictures and personal effects—even his favourite armchair in the library—and you had Lachie put it all out of sight in the shed.' He shook his head at the futility. 'Doing that won't help you, Shona. And you can't even escape by coming here. He dominated you all your life and he's still doing it. You need help, Shona, and that's why I'm here.'

Her throat tightened again. Did a fool like her really deserve a man like him? Time and time again he'd proved his love for her, and she'd treated him abominably.

Bowing her head in shame, she made her admission in a low, tortured voice, 'I ... I just can't help it, Dirk. I know it must sound ridiculous to you. I mean ... I owe him nothing, yet I've still got this terrible feeling that I'm doing wrong by him and letting him down.'

Dirk's hand squeezed her shoulder gently. 'I understand. Perhaps better than you know.'

'How can you?' She raised her despair-laden eyes. 'It doesn't make sense, even to me. Why should I be the one to feel guilty? And if it isn't my conscience that's bothering me, then what is it? Why do I feel like this, Dirk?'

He gave his answer in a voice which was sharp enough to cut through her shroud of self-pity and drive the point home once and for all. 'It's because your subconscious mind still can't believe that he used you for his own selfish ends. That's what I mean by going back and facing him. If you do that you'll finally be facing the truth and you'll have no option but to accept it. Then and only then will you stop feeling guilty. You'll be able to shift it on to his shoulders where it belongs. It's the only way.'

She took in what he said, but doubt still clouded her eyes. 'That all sounds very sensible, darling, and I know that I should believe it. So why do I think that he's still going to put a curse on us the day we marry?' She laughed harshly. 'Will you just listen to the way I'm talking? I'm supposed to be educated and I'm standing here talking about curses from the grave. Are you still sure that you want to marry an idiot like me, Dirk?'

He laid down his coffee and took her firmly in his arms. 'What other kind of wife do you think I'd want? Some vacant-eyed fool with a painted smile and a cabbage for a brain?' He stroked her hair gently. 'You and I are two of a kind, Shona. The same Celtic blood runs in our veins. This is the land of fairies and witches and dark deeds. We were brought up on that folklore. We absorbed it with our mother's milk. We don't admit it, but deep in all our poetic souls we're not so far removed from our pagan ancestors.'

She swallowed. 'That kind of talk scares me, Dirk. I wish you'd stop it.'

He held her tighter. 'You've nothing to be frightened of. I'm here to protect you.' He paused, then looked down at her with a glint of humour in his eyes. 'What we need is an exorcism.'

She shivered in his arms. 'I told you to stop talking like that.'

'And I'm telling you to trust me,' he said firmly. 'You wouldn't want to marry a man you couldn't trust, would you?'

She hadn't the faintest idea of what he had in mind, and she had her misgivings, but in spite of that she managed a smile. 'Of course I trust you.'

'Good.' He gave her a final lingering kiss then said, 'We'll go and pay Rory a visit and I'll have a talk with him. We'll get this mess sorted out once and for all.'

'You're going to talk to Rory?' She eyed him uncertainly. 'How do you intend doing that?'

'Just you leave that to me.' He pointed towards the river. 'Go and collect some wild flowers and we'll take them to the churchyard.'

They went in his Land Rover up across the high moor and then down into Kinvaig. Opposite the hotel a narrow road led uphill towards the church, and Dirk parked the Land Rover by the gates.

Bemused, and nervously clutching the wild flowers she'd collected in the Glen, she led the way past the well tended plots to a lonely and secluded corner where a polished granite headstone marked her father's resting place. The Reverend Mr MacLeod had told her that Rory had chosen this spot himself.

Kneeling down, she carefully arranged the flowers, then closed her eyes for a few moments. In the silence all she could hear was the heavy beating of her own heart, and she whispered, 'I'm going to try to forgive you, Father, and you're going to have to forgive me for going against your wishes. Dirk's a good man and we'll give you grandchildren you can be proud of.'

Dirk helped her gently to her feet, then gave her a comforting smile before glaring at the headstone. 'Aye, Rory,' he drawled insolently. 'It's me. Dirk

MacAllister. Now there's no use lying down there shaking your fist at me and calling me names. It won't do you any good. Shona and I are going to get married and there's not a damned thing you can do about it.' Taking her hand in his, he clasped it tightly then addressed the headstone again. 'You can see for yourself that we love one another, so I've come here to tell you to leave her in peace and let us get on with our lives. I've told her what really happened that night, so now she knows how you tricked her.'

She bit her lip and began to feel distinctly uncomfortable. There was something slightly distasteful about this, and she tugged her hand free. 'Dirk! This is silly. Let's go.'

He looked down at her in disappointment for a moment, then he gave an understanding smile. 'Perhaps you should wait by the Land Rover. I'm not finished yet.'

Embarrassed and a little confused, she trudged back to the gate, then watched as Dirk carried on his animated conversation with the headstone. Shaking her head in despair, she waited in silent agitation. Whispering a prayer by a grave was one thing, but standing there talking to yourself was something else. What did he think he was playing at? Whatever it was it certainly wasn't doing anything for her peace of mind.

At long last he rejoined her and said briskly, 'Well, that's all been taken care of now. He'll give you no trouble from now on. Now I think this calls for a celebratory drink in the hotel. We can announce our engagement while we're there.'

She sat tight-lipped with her arms folded until he parked outside the hotel, then she looked at him angrily. 'What was the meaning of all that? If anyone else had seen you you'd have been locked up.'

He raised an eyebrow in surprise at her outburst. 'Why? Is there a law against talking to ghosts?'

'Don't try to be smart with me,' she snapped. 'I know why you staged that little exhibition. You just wanted to show me how stupid I'm being about my fears.' She sniffed. 'There was no need to go to the lengths you did.'

He sighed. 'I thought I was doing you a favour. Anyway, he's agreed to let you go ahead and marry me on one condition.'

She donned an expression of weariness. She'd go along with this foolishness if it kept him happy. 'All right. I give in. What condition?'

'He wants us to name his first grandson Rory. As a gesture of respect.'

She shrugged and managed to keep a straight face. 'And what did you tell him?'

'I told him that it was entirely up to you. I've no objections.' He paused thoughtfully then said, 'To tell the truth, I think it was my threat that really did the trick.'

She looked at him closely and noticed for the first time the wicked gleam of amusement in his eyes. There was some reason behind all this, but she couldn't imagine what. Continuing with the charade, she said, 'You actually threatened him? How did you manage that?'

His voice took on a matter-of-fact tone that made what he was saying sound utterly convincing. 'Well, we were chatting about this and that and so forth and I asked him how he liked being on his own in a quiet corner of the graveyard. Rory said that he liked it fine.

It was a nice sunny spot. In the summer the view was nice and in the winter the drystone dike kept the worst of the wind away. I asked him if he'd like some company, someone to chat to whenever he felt lonely, and he said he damned well wouldn't. He liked things just the way they were. So I said that that was too bad because I was thinking of having my own father moved next to him. I told him that Blackie was getting fed up with young courting couples leaving crisp packets and empty cans of Coke at the foot of his headstone. "Bloody undignified" he called it.'

'So what did Rory say to that?' she asked, desperately trying to keep her face straight.

'Well, I wouldn't like to repeat it in front of a lady, but in the end he could see that I meant business. That's when he made the condition about calling our first son after him. At least it would be one in the eye for Blackie, he said.'

Shona nodded gravely. 'I see. And did you tell him how mad I am at him for all the trouble he caused?'

'Don't worry. He knows how you feel and I've to tell you that he's sorry. He was only doing what he thought was best at the time. Anyway, just before I left him he wished us both the best of luck and told me we were to call on him any time we were passing. Oh ... and we've to tell MacLeod to get someone to cut the bloody grass now and again.'

She quickly undid her seatbelt and got out to find that her legs were shaking. In fact everything was shaking, and Dirk put his arm around her for support. Looking up at him, she suddenly burst into laughter. 'How can I ever take anything you say seriously again?'

He grinned. 'I'm only serious about the things that really matter. Our life together, for one thing.'

Her throat began to tighten again and she felt her heart melting with an all-consuming love. She'd been a child, afraid of the dark, but not any longer.

It was late evening and the sun was low in the western sky when they returned to Glen Gallan to collect her jeep.

Dirk had been quiet and thoughtful during the drive over the moor, and now he was striding purposefully around the ground downriver from the chalet while she sat on the veranda steps with her chin in her hand.

She had no idea what he was up to, but no doubt he would tell her in his own good time. Meanwhile she smiled contentedly as she reviewed the events of the day.

Any other man, less patient, might have scoffed and derided or got angry at her irrational fear, but Dirk had turned her fear into laughter, and for that alone she would be eternally grateful. When she'd recovered her composure sufficiently he'd led her into the hotel bar and announced their forthcoming wedding to the astonished customers. The local bush telegraph had immediately sprung into action just as they'd known it would. Boats were hurriedly tied up at the pier and the crews scrambled ashore. Shutters went up on the shops. Lachie was contacted on the CB and told to fetch Mrs Ross and Morag, and the ceilidh started in earnest. Remembering the last one, she'd stuck to orange juice this time.

As she watched Dirk now she recalled that day so long ago when she'd first met him after her return from university. She'd been so young and innocent.

She recalled the way the wind had moulded her thin cotton dress to her body and the way her embarrassment had vanished when she'd seen the look of pleasure and admiration in his eyes. Instinctively she'd felt that her whole purpose in being born was simply to please him. When he'd touched her bare arm the gentle contact of his fingers had sent shivers of excitement through her body. No other man had ever had that effect on her and no other man ever would. At that moment she'd known that she was his woman.

When she'd surrendered and revelled in his passionate lovemaking that same day on Para Mhor it had been the revelation of a new dimension to life. It was a dimension she'd only read about or heard about second-hand, and nothing had prepared her for the reality. It had been much more than sex—a union of bodies. She'd felt that their very souls had touched and shared a wonderful experience that day. Was that the real definition of love?

And then it had all gone wrong, but perhaps, in a way, the bond between them had been tested and strengthened. Rather than wound her by destroying her love for her father, he'd shouldered all the blame and suffered the harsh words of her anger and contempt. At that moment he could so easily have given up, cast her aside, and sought love somewhere else, but he hadn't. No man could have done more to prove his love than he had.

She straightened up and got to her feet as she saw him make his way back to the chalet.

'I've found it,' he announced with an air of satisfaction. 'Take my hand and I'll show you.'

Like a pair of teenage lovers they walked hand in hand down the riverside until they reached the spot he'd been so patiently surveying. 'Our house will be here,' he told her. 'What do you think?'

Her blue eyes widened in excitement. 'We're actually going to live here?'

'It's what you want, isn't it?' he asked softly.

'Oh, yes, darling,' she breathed. 'But I never for one moment believed it would ever be possible.'

'From now on anything is possible.' He gazed down into her eyes, pleased at her reaction to his news. 'I know a good architect in Glasgow. We'll fetch him up here and have him design it. You and Morag can contribute your own ideas.'

Suddenly a tiny frown creased her brow. 'If Morag is going to be our housekeeper what are you going to do about Mrs Ross? She won't be retiring for a few years yet.'

'I thought about that a long time ago,' he assured her with a smile. 'I was going to build an extension to the hotel for the extra summer visitors we'll be getting, but I've decided to convert some of the old property in the village into a guest-house. Mrs Ross will be happy to take care of that.'

She stood on tiptoe and kissed him. 'You've thought of everything, haven't you? Tell me ... how many children are we going to have?'

His hands slipped round her waist, pulling her gently closer. 'How many would you like?'

'Three or four at least,' she murmured. 'We've got to make sure that the Struan MacAllisters get off to a good start. I want Glen Gallan to be the birthplace of a new dynasty. Do you think we can manage that?'

His lips nuzzled at her ear. 'Easily. Two sons to start with, then two daughters to follow. And a long time from now, when we're sitting in our rocking-chairs, we'll be surrounded by our great-grandchildren.'

Her hands slid under his jacket and T-shirt and rubbed sensuously at his back and shoulders, feeling the hard strength beneath the smooth, warm flesh. 'It's getting late,' she whispered. 'I don't like driving over the high moor at night. The road is too rough.'

He nodded and smiled with amusement and anticipation. 'Aye. You're right. It would be far too dangerous. What do you suggest?'

'Well,' she breathed softly, 'it would be far more sensible to stay the night here and go back in the morning.'

His arms pulled her even closer and she could feel his own desire thrusting against her. 'I think that's a very good idea, darling,' he said.

As they walked slowly towards the chalet the dying rays of the sun sent their long shadows racing impatiently ahead. For a moment the steep sides of the Glen flared from golden to red then to deep purple. From the sea came a gentle cleansing breeze to stir the grass and the leaves of the birches and to sweep away the ghosts and memories of the past. The first star of the evening appeared.

They both paused on the veranda for a moment to gaze in wonder at the beauty of it all, then gently he lifted her into his arms and carried her inside.

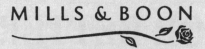

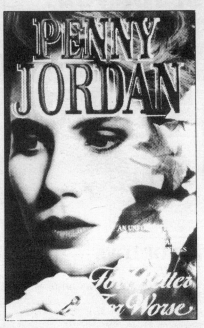

4 FREE

Romances and 2 FREE gifts just for you!

You can enjoy all the heartwarming emotion of true love for FREE! Discover the heartbreak and happiness, the emotion and the tenderness of the modern relationships in Mills & Boon Romances.

We'll send you 4 Romances as a special offer from Mills & Boon Reader Service, along with the opportunity to have 6 captivating new Romances delivered to your door each month.

Claim your FREE books and gifts overleaf...

An irresistible offer from Mills & Boon

Become a regular reader of Romances with Mills & Boon Reader Service and we'll welcome you with 4 books, a CUDDLY TEDDY and a special MYSTERY GIFT all absolutely FREE.

And then look forward to receiving 6 brand new Romances each month, delivered to your door hot off the presses, postage and packing FREE! Plus our free Newsletter featuring author news, competitions, special offers and much more.

This invitation comes with no strings attached. You may cancel or suspend your subscription at any time, and still keep your free books and gifts.

It's so easy. Send no money now. Simply fill in the coupon below and post it to -
Reader Service, FREEPOST, PO Box 236, Croydon, Surrey CR9 9EL.

NO STAMP REQUIRED

Free Books Coupon

Yes! Please rush me 4 FREE Romances and 2 FREE gifts! Please also reserve me a Reader Service subscription. If I decide to subscribe I can look forward to receiving 6 brand new Romances for just £10.80 each month, postage and packing FREE. If I decide not to subscribe I shall write to you within 10 days - I can keep the free books and gifts whatever I choose. I may cancel or suspend my subscription at any time. I am over 18 years of age.

Ms/Mrs/Miss/Mr _____ EP56R

Address _____

_____

Postcode _____ Signature _____

Offers closes 31st March 1994. The right is reserved to refuse an application and change the terms of this offer. This offer does not apply to Romance subscribers. One application per household. Overseas readers please write for details. Southern Africa write to Book Services International Ltd., Box 41654, Craighall, Transvaal 2024. You may be mailed with offers from other reputable companies as a result of this application. Please tick box if you would prefer not to receive such offers. ☐

mps MAILING PREFERENC SERVICE

ESCAPE INTO ANOTHER WORLD...

...With Temptation Dreamscape Romances

Two worlds collide in 3 very special Temptation titles, guaranteed to sweep you to the very edge of reality.

The timeless mysteries of reincarnation, telepathy and earthbound spirits clash with the modern lives and passions of ordinary men and women.

Available November 1993   Price £5.55

MILLS & BOON

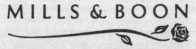

Next Month's Romances

Each month you can choose from a wide variety of romance with Mills & Boon. Below are the new titles to look out for next month, why not ask either Mills & Boon Reader Service or your Newsagent to reserve you a copy of the titles you want to buy – just tick the titles you would like and either post to Reader Service or take it to any Newsagent and ask them to order your books.

Please save me the following titles:	Please tick	√
UNWILLING MISTRESS	Lindsay Armstrong	
DARK HERITAGE	Emma Darcy	
WOUNDS OF PASSION	Charlotte Lamb	
LOST IN LOVE	Michelle Reid	
ORIGINAL SIN	Rosalie Ash	
SUDDEN FIRE	Elizabeth Oldfield	
THE BRIDE OF SANTA BARBARA	Angela Devine	
ISLAND OF SHELLS	Grace Green	
LOVE'S REVENGE	Mary Lyons	
MAKING MAGIC	Karen van der Zee	
OASIS OF THE HEART	Jessica Hart	
BUILD A DREAM	Quinn Wilder	
A BRIDE TO LOVE	Barbara McMahon	
A MAN CALLED TRAVERS	Brittany Young	
A CHILD CALLED MATTHEW	Sara Grant	
DANCE OF SEDUCTION	Vanessa Grant	

If you would like to order these books in addition to your regular subscription from Mills & Boon Reader Service please send £1.80 per title to: Mills & Boon Reader Service, Freepost, P.O. Box 236, Croydon, Surrey, CR9 9EL, quote your Subscriber No:.................................... (If applicable) and complete the name and address details below. Alternatively, these books are available from many local Newsagents including W.H.Smith, J.Menzies, Martins and other paperback stockists from 14 January 1994.

Name:...

Address:...

....Post Code:..........................

To Retailer: If you would like to stock M&B books please contact your regular book/magazine wholesaler for details.